W9-BTB-899

Dry Souls

Denise Getson

CBAY BOOKS
Austin, Texas

For Miss Judy Fowler,
Frazier Elementary,
who nudged me in the right direction.
And for all the wonderful teachers after-
ward who encouraged me to find my voice.

Dry Souls
By Denise Getson

Copyright © 2011 by Denise Getson.
All rights reserved. Except where permitted under
the U.S. Copyright Act of 1976, no part of this
publication may be reproduced, distributed, or
transmitted in any form or by any means includ-
ing but not limited to storage in a database or
retrieval system or online in any way without the
prior written consent of the publisher.

Children's Brains are Yummy Books
(CBAY Books)
PO Box 92411
Austin, TX 78709

Visit our website at www.cbaybooks.com

The characters and events in this book are purely
fictitious. Any similarity to real persons, living
or dead, is coincidental and not intended by the
author.

Printed in the United States of America.
For more information on CPSIA compliance go to
www.cbaybooks.com/cpsia.html

So let man consider of what he was created;
he was created of gushing water
issuing between the loins and the breast-bones.
— Qur'an, "The Night-Star," 86:5-7

1

I glance at the sky, but there are no clouds. There are never clouds. I know what clouds look like only because of the digital images in our lessons at school. I know someone who has been north, to the mountains, and swears she saw clouds. Perhaps she's telling the truth, but I doubt it.

I take my book to a spot I like, a quiet corner behind the shed. There's shade here. The ground is hard and cracked, separated into rough-edged shards that can pierce the skin, but I bring a cushion with me.

I'm reading a book about flowers. I don't have much personal experience with flowers. It's against the law to have unauthorized vegetation on private property. Plants require so much water, you see, that every kind of gardening or agriculture must be approved by the proper agencies.

Naturally, we don't have much in the way of plant life here at the orphanage. We have cactus, the tall and the short kind, creating an obstacle course of pincushions throughout the property, and a tomato patch was approved after proper petitioning by Matron. When the fruit's ripe, we have fresh tomatoes with every meal, which is a treat.

But flowers are considered a frivolous use of water. Flowers—the purely ornamental kind—are non-essential. However, I've discovered a flower tucked into a small patch of earth behind the shed. No one ever comes here but me, and I don't think it's been discovered. It should have died by now since summer is full upon us and the heat is fierce, but I've been watering it in secret.

Every night, instead of drinking my last ration of water, I save a swallow in my mouth. Discreetly, I slip out of the dining room. I go to our sleeping quarters and spit the water into a small, covered dish I keep beneath my bed. Every few days, when I have a break from my studies and my chores, I take the water to the shed and pour it out onto the ground.

The flower's beautiful. The blossoms are small and pink and clustered together like tiny bells. The petals are softer than anything I've ever felt in my life. I touch one now, for the pure pleasure of it, before getting comfortable on the cushion and opening my book.

I want to find out what kind of flower I have. The book hints it might be a variety of bluebell, except that my flower is not blue, or even purple, as most bluebells were. It is clearly pink.

"What are you doing back here?"

I freeze, my breath catching at the back of my throat. Carefully, I lean back until I'm sure no part of the flower can be seen. Placing one finger on the page to hold my spot, I glance up.

"What does it look like I'm doing?"

I'm not in the habit of making nice with Mary Castle, but neither am I in the habit of being deliberately difficult. I try for casual disinterest and gaze at my intruder with what I hope is just the right mixture of impatience and preoccupation. Looking at Mary always makes me feel impatient, anyway. She's too perfect, too put-together. Whenever I see her, I want to rumple her up.

Mary studies the book in my lap then raises one snooty eyebrow. "You're wasting your time studying flowers," she snorts. "You might as well be studying Latin or some other useless thing."

"It's my personal time. I'll read whatever I want."

"Matron wants you inside. Visitors are coming tomorrow. You and Sheila have floors."

I hide my dismay. No one wants floors. Matron insists we get on our hands and knees, running a cloth over every hard square inch. I know I'll be aching from it tomorrow. Still, I won't let Mary see that I care one way or the other. She's probably the one who suggested me for the stupid job in the first place.

"What are you waiting for?" she snaps. "Let's go."

I hold my position, keeping my gaze on hers. "I'll be there in a minute."

"Matron doesn't like to be kept waiting."

"Beat it."

Mary narrows her eyes, looks as though she's going to say something then shrugs. With a wrinkle of her delicate nose, she heads back to the house, leaving me alone in the shadow of the outbuilding.

I exhale as tension seeps from my body. Slowly, I close my book, listening for any sound that indicates someone else might be nearby. I pick up the dish lying on the ground beside me and stand, peering around the corner. All's clear.

"Aha!"

I turn, startled, as Mary steps around the opposite corner. Darn that girl for a sneak! My mind's racing, trying to think of a way to divert her attention.

"I told you to beat it!" I growl, getting in her face, my free hand fisted and ready to swing. I honestly don't know if Mary can take a punch, but we're about to find out.

"Why are you always hiding back here?"

"I'm not hiding. It's just...I like it. It's private." I stare at her pointedly. "Most of the time that is."

"What's that?"

"What?"

"In your hand."

I glance at the dish in my hand, then down at the lid lying on the ground next to my flower.

"What've you got in there?" She reaches, grabbing the small bowl from my grasp. I swing my arm to take it back, but she holds it just out of reach. She tips the container up and catches the lone, last drop onto her face. "It's water." She turns accusing eyes to mine. "Where did you get this? You've been stealing!"

"I have not! I mean," I struggle to keep my voice

4

even, "that water was *my* water, part of my ration. I've just been saving a bit to…uh…so I could have a sip when I'm out here reading, that's all. It gets hot." I hold out my hand. "Now, give it back."

She looks at me suspiciously, but slowly, her arm comes down and with it my bowl. I step forward to take it from her and at that moment, something happens. Mary's eyes shift from mine to a space just beyond where I was standing.

The dish falls into my hand, but Mary's already pushed past me, her eyes wide on the ground by the shed. My heart sinks. I turn around, silent.

"Is that a real flower?" She lifts her face to mine, her features stark with amazement.

I watch as Mary turns astonished eyes back to the ground. She bends down and puts out a finger to gently tap one of the soft bells. I want to shout and grab her arm. It's my flower! But, I wait. I watch as she strokes the delicate pink, then looks at me with damp eyes. Ah, geez. Is she crying?

"I won't tell a soul, Kira. I swear."

My jaw drops open in disbelief and I close it with a snap. Does she mean it? After a minute, I nod slowly. She gives me a hesitant look.

"Do you think it would be alright if I come out here sometimes? I mean, I know this is your special place, but…when you're not using it, you know. I could maybe save some of my water, too."

My first instinct is to tell her to get lost. This is my spot. But, I can't undo her knowing about the flower.

5

Clearly, I have to get her on my side. Besides, with two of us watering it, there might be a chance to save it. Who knows? Maybe next spring, we'll have two flowers.

"I guess that would be alright," I say finally, rocking back on my heels. I try for just the right touch of nonchalance. "But don't be obvious about it. I don't want Matron getting suspicious."

"I promise." She gives me a watery smile, glances at the flower, then leaves.

As soon as she's gone, I sink down onto my cushion with a trembling breath. I can't believe it. Mary's going to help me take care of the flower. That's a surprise. Still, I have to be careful. One of the other girls might wander back here and not be as good about it as Mary was. I shake my head, still trying to wrap my mind around what's happened. She seemed honestly moved by the flower.

Of course, water's going to be a problem. Even with Mary and me saving our spit, the hottest weather's still to come.

I bend over the tiny blossoms. "I wish I could make it easier," I whisper. "I wish I could make water for you, right here; right now."

Then, it happens.

I don't see it at first. I'm concentrating on the flower, placing a finger against the arc of the stem to test its strength. My eye is caught by a small patch of dirt that's suddenly darker than the rest. I put my finger to the ground and feel. It's damp. As I watch, a small puddle appears. Water trickles up out of the ground. The puddle spreads to the base of the flower then stops.

I blink slowly, pressing my hand to my head. I'm not sure what just happened. I stand up, still staring at the ground. The sun's hot today and I've been out for awhile. I don't think I applied my sun block as thoroughly as I should have. Mental confusion and hallucinations are common sunstroke symptoms. Every school child knows that. Sunstroke. That must be it. I need to get out of the heat and hydrate. Leaving my cushion and dish, I head back to the house in a daze, shielding my face from the sun.

2

"Hey, Kira, is it true your mother was a freak?"

I stop in my tracks, glad the girl behind me can't see my skin flush. I don't have to turn around to know who's taunting me. Casually, I relax my body into a fighting stance.

"Hey, Crystal," I respond softly. "I heard your mother's still alive. You're here because she didn't *want* you."

The hiss behind me has my hands clenching. I twirl, just in time to meet Crystal's right hook. I'm momentarily stunned, my eyes filling with unwanted tears, my head snapping from the impact. I should have been prepared. Crystal always goes for the right hook. A red film drops across my vision, and then I'm barreling into the other girl, my punches aimed at the soft targets I know will hurt her more and me less. Immediately, there are a half dozen girls joining in the fray. I feel my fist connect with bone—I'm not sure whose—and hear the sudden "oomph" of air being expelled when I lower my head and ram into someone's gut.

I'm not unhurt. In a vague, distant sort of way, I'm aware of the taste of blood in my mouth and something's not right with my left leg. Has it been kicked or twisted? It doesn't matter. I know the pain will come later.

My lungs are empty of air, and it feels like I've been fighting forever, but it's probably only minutes before Matron strides over, grabbing ears and arms and peeling bodies apart.

I never get the chance to tell my side of the story. Six sets of fingers point at me along with a chorus of "Kira started it." Matron puts a tight grip on my shoulder and propels me into her office. I turn and rake Crystal with one last scorching glance. "My mother was *not* a freak," I whisper for her ears only. Then I shrug off Matron's hand and march inside.

Matron's office gives me the creeps. Well, it's not her office so much. It's the painting hanging behind her desk. The Garner Home for Girls is just that—a home for girls. Even the staff is all female. So, the portrait of the large mustached man that dominates Matron's office seems out of place.

"Do you want to explain yourself?"

Matron's voice has me pulling my eyes away from the painting to the woman behind the desk. There's nothing matronly about her, certainly nothing maternal. She is stiff and stern, and her voice is gravelly when she speaks.

"No ma'am."

Her fingers drum on the tabletop, creating a matching rhythm inside me. I want to grab her hand and smash it flat, but I force myself to sit quietly.

"I'm running out of punishments, Kira, and I'm

running out of patience. You know, there are other places for people like you—places which would treat you a lot less kindly than we do at the Garner Home."

My fingers twitch on the arms of my chair. "What do you mean 'people like me?'"

She looks momentarily at a loss, but recovers. "You're touchy, Kira. You take things too personally."

"I do not!"

Matron gazes at me mildly.

I blow my bangs in frustration. "I just take things personally when they're meant personally, that's all."

"Kira, you have to learn to get along with others. I'm giving you one more chance to improve your behavior. If you can't shape up, I'm going to suggest you for a transfer to one of the vocational homes."

I stay silent, refusing to cave in to her intimidation. I know I'm not like the other girls, and I don't care. I don't like to do the things they do. I don't care about the same things. But, I'm not a troublemaker. At least, not intentionally. I keep my face blank.

"Fine," Matron mutters, becoming businesslike. "For the next two weeks, you can help Cook in the kitchen. You'll be responsible for breakfast and dinner."

"Geez Louise! Breakfast *and* dinner!"

"I can still add lunch, if you like," she says calmly.

I cross my arms, biting my tongue so hard, I'm sure to have permanent teeth marks. Immediately, I begin plotting how I can sprinkle ash on Crystal's seaweed, in place of pepper. The image of Crystal gagging on her first bite has me feeling better.

"I don't know what you're smiling about, young lady, but whatever it is, I'd rethink it if I were you."

Matron's eyes are narrowed on my face. Quickly, I compose my features into an expression of meekness. She raises one disbelieving brow and, with a tired wave of her hand, motions me out of the room. I jump up, eager to get back to my own quarters.

The girls at the Garner Home live in long sleeping rooms according to our age group. At sixteen, I've recently graduated to the upperclassmen's quarters. In a year, I'll have to decide whether to apply to one of the technical schools or get a work assignment, but I'm in no hurry. It can be foolish to think too much about a future that's uncertain. Better to take things one day at a time.

The sleeping quarters are silent. At this time of the day, everyone's in the main building, doing homework or doing chores. I slip my hand beneath my pillow and pull out a small photograph. Stepping over to a mirror on the wall, I hold the picture beside my face. The familiar image stares back at me through the glass. There's a resemblance. Round grey eyes stare into round grey eyes. But where my hair is cropped and smooth and red in the light, my mother's is dark and wavy, capturing the light and holding it.

I don't know where the rumor about my mother started, but it's been floating around as long as I can remember. Maybe Matron knew her before she died, but she's never said, and I refuse to ask. My own memories are thin and wispy, hard to hold onto except in that

11

moment just before waking.

I stick out my tongue at my reflection, then turn and slip the photo back beneath my pillow. I have a meal to prepare. I smile briefly in anticipation before leaving the room.

3

Mary's true to her word. I'm skeptical at first, but soon I realize this flower is a small miracle, and it's made a miracle in our lives. She and I make peace, working together to create a schedule of times when we'll water the flower.

We take turns carrying our small containers of water out back. Although there're now two of us watering the flower, it's getting harder to keep it alive. The sun creates tiny heat explosions in my head every time I walk outside. One hundred and fifteen degree days are not uncommon. Even with a lavish layer of sun protection, I wilt in the summer heat. I don't know how my flower bears it.

I understand why the flowers disappeared. After the Devastation, a lot of things disappeared, or they changed into something unrecognizable from what they'd been. People saved some things: vines that flowered and turned into squash or beans or melons. They were saved. Agricultural production became limited to Biospheres only, where soil and air conditions could be closely monitored.

Of course, everyone has a mail order algae tank, complete with rotors and evaporation shields and solar panels, algae being one life form that has no problem growing in the harshest of environments. The harvesting cycle for algae is less than ten days, so we never run out. I don't know if we could survive without a constant supply of the stuff.

Flowers, however, are another matter. Flowers that were just flowers—flowers that didn't turn into food—gradually vanished. It's as if they sensed they were no longer appreciated and collectively decided to disappear from the earth.

I hear stories. Travelers come through and tell us about places where things still grow, even without human intervention. One old man said he'd seen roses. They hadn't smelled like much, he said, not like you'd expect a rose to smell, but they were roses all the same. I'd like to see roses.

Of course, wanting to see roses is impractical. I know that. And above all, the Garner Home for Girls is a very practical place. The staff are real nuts-and-bolts types, determined to teach us the lessons we need to get by in a dying world.

In the upper classes, sometimes the computers teach us and sometimes Matron does. She pulls down maps showing all the places I've never seen, the territories around Xeta and the Biospheres, where most of our food is grown and our clothes manufactured.

History class is my favorite. Last week I learned that before the Devastation, before the chemicals got deep inside us and the planet heated up, people used to worry because they were fat. Isn't that funny? For all the problems the Devastation brought, it solved that one. From the youngest child to the oldest citizen—and there are few among us who are truly old—everyone is lean and dry and weathered to a dusty brown, just like the landscape.

"What's with you two?"

"What?"

I frown at the group of girls standing in front of me and Mary. The noise level in the common room tapers off as heads turn our way.

"What's with you two sitting over here being all chummy all of a sudden?" Crystal glares at us, her eyes moving from Mary to me.

I suppose it was only a question of time until we were confronted. Until Mary and I started sharing responsibility for the flower, no one talked to me much. It wasn't like I cared, I told myself. I preferred my own company to the senseless chatter of the other girls. But, well, things are different now. "We're just..." my mind scrambling, I glance at Mary.

"We've found a common interest," she says quickly. "That's all."

Thank goodness Mary's got her wits about her, "It turns out, we're both fascinated by...um..." I grab a book from a pile on the table. "Xeta history."

Mary shoots me an incredulous look then nods vigorously. "That's it," she says, "Xeta history."

Crystal and her friends look disbelieving. I don't

blame them. From the time we were children, Mary and I have had as little to do with each other as possible. We were resentful of each other's qualities. I have admitted to her my resentment toward her appearance. Her skin is a little too clear, her hair too fine and glossy; her manner too vain. She has admitted that she resented my marks in class, my solitary nature; my tendency to punch first and ask questions later. We're over it now.

The girls stand there, staring at us. We stare back, our eyes wide and innocent. When Matron pokes her head into the room, they grumble and wander off, but I can tell they're suspicious. This is the last thing we need.

With the prospect of confrontation removed, the other girls resume their conversations. Mary bends her head close to mine. "Do you think they'll leave us alone?" she whispers.

"It's probably a good idea to be on our guard," I warn. "Don't trust anybody."

"Right."

She gets up and heads for the kitchen, and I sit there, staring at the wall. I haven't told Mary about that moment behind the shed. Why would I? Surely, I imagined the whole thing. I haven't tried to wish for water again either, but suddenly it's urgent that I do. Was it really a hallucination? Or maybe I'm coming down with something, something toxic and deadly. I shudder, remembering the girl last year who fainted one day in the middle of science class and never woke up.

Cautiously, I glance around the room. Everyone's occupied, wrapped in their activities. Crystal and her crowd have gone to their quarters. I slip out of the room unnoticed and head out back.

Xeta is a landscape with a subtle palette. The outbuilding stands stark against a large sky. The colors of brown and beige and tan and every variation in-between fill my eyes. When everything is always brown, brown, brown, a splash of pink can be a wondrous thing.

I take a furtive look around, then turn the corner and drop to the ground to check the flower. The leaves have curled up and the green edges are starting to crisp. It's heartbreaking. I can almost feel its struggle.

I quell the butterflies in my stomach. Okay. Here goes. I take a deep breath and close my eyes. "I wish for water," I whisper. I open my eyes and glance at the ground. Nothing. Nothing moves. Nothing appears. All is as it should be, brown and dry. I relax, sitting back on my heels in relief and give a soft laugh. It's nothing after all. Then suddenly, it's there, a dark stain growing against the dirt, soaking up the top layer of soil, working its way around the base of my flower's green stem.

I collapse against the wall, my eyes fixed on the small puddle. What is wrong with me?

The next couple of days I spend in a vacuum, numbly going about my daily routine. I don't notice what I eat or who I'm speaking to or who speaks to me.

I stop saving my spit. The container beneath my bed stands empty. There no longer seems a reason to hack up my saliva when I can water the flower at will.

But where does the water come from?

I have no idea, and it worries me. Water can't be conjured out of thin air. It has to come from somewhere. I draw it up out of...what? Some deep reservoir, perhaps? That doesn't make sense. Every hidden spring and aquifer has long since been uncovered by technology.

Do I draw it from the sky? I stare upward, but the sky's cloudless as always. Maybe the Garner Home for Girls rests on a bridge between our world and a parallel universe, and I'm drawing water from the other side. I laugh weakly. Yeah, right.

Mary watches me with worried eyes. I see her holding her swallow of water at the end of each day, then slipping out of the room to spit into her jar.

I'm still in a worried funk when a traveler shows up at the door of the Garner Home, requesting a meal and water in exchange for repairs to our outbuildings. Travelers are a rare and resilient breed, men and women who walk from one outpost to the next, driven by something inside them that won't let them sit still. Travelers are especially short-lived, constantly exposed to toxic areas and to the threat of dehydration. I think they prefer it that way, living life on the edge.

As discreetly as I can, I watch him throughout the day: repairing a screen, reattaching loose molding, cleaning the rotors in the algae pond. His features are tired and weathered, but kind. Once, I bring him a glass of water from Matron, and he thanks me. I heave a huge sigh of relief when none of his repairs take him behind the shed. At the end of the day, he joins us at the table for dinner. He eats with relish, his attention concentrated on his food, before leaning back in his chair to tell us about the places he's been; the boundaries he's crossed. Crystal is openly disbelieving.

"It's impossible to get through Delta Territory on

foot," she says, her tone filled with scorn. "Everyone knows that territory is completely toxic."

The leathery man laughs.

"It's hard," he concedes dryly. "But not impossible."

Delta Territory is where I was born. I know that much. My mom died there. Somewhere. And Crystal is right. Everyone knows it's completely toxic.

All evening, I listen avidly to his stories about criss-crossing the 'Big Dry', the travelers' term for the draught-stricken lands of the unified territories. His tales are full of unyielding landscapes and resilient peoples.

"Why do you travel?" I ask, staring into his eyes, trying to make sense of the strange light there that, even in this small room, seems to look beyond concrete walls to some greater spaciousness beyond.

"I travel to find the place where the Earth remembers."

"Remembers what?"

"Remembers what it used to be," he says softly, his eyes calm.

Crystal snorts. "I've heard this garbage before. It's a fairytale for children. There's no such place."

"Where is it?" I ask the man.

He scans the faces in the room, his eyes moving slowly from one girl to the next. My skin is tingling and I'm holding my breath. I resist the urge to stamp my foot, impatient for his answer.

"No one knows," he says finally, his words sending a wave of desolation through me. He swings his eyes back to mine. Perhaps he senses my feelings of hopelessness. His gaze bores into mine with grave intensity, as though he were trying to convince me of this place through the sheer force of his will. "It's not a place on any map, but it exists. I believe it. I *know* it."

"Why are you so sure?"

"Think about your own mind inside you," he says, reaching over to tap gently on my forehead. "What's there? Grey matter, right? Just like the land around us. But there are also memories, bright and poignant places that live inside you. You feel them, you can relive the experiences in vibrant, sensory detail, but you can't map them on your brain. You just know they're in there. It's like that."

"But the earth isn't alive."

"It's dying, yes, but it's not gone yet. And neither are we. We're all constructed of the same stuff, you know. Atoms and molecules and invisible subatomic particles that animate us, that animate the world. We're all vibrating pieces of the universe. Even the iron in your blood comes from supernovas, those brilliant blasts of elements that formed the basis for all life. That's real. And it binds us together in ways that are invisible to the human eye. The earth and the people on it, we're all connected."

His words leave me confused. I have no reason to believe in any of this. It's foolish and fanciful and, these days, a girl needs to keep her wits about her. But just for a moment, I suspend my disbelief and let myself imagine that such a thing is possible. Because it makes sense to me. Everything I know evolved from this earth and on it. And a tiny cell can't see the whole body, can't see how it all works together. And maybe the earth does have a sort of consciousness, and memories, good memories somewhere that survive.

The traveler wipes his mouth and stands. "Now ladies, the sun is going down and I need to hit the road. This is the best time for walking. I greatly appreciate the meal and the company."

He shakes hands with each one of us, even Crystal, and says a polite good-bye. His grip feels warm and solid and, even though I don't know this man, I'm sorry to see him leave. As soon as he's gone, I slip out of the room. Mary corners me in the hallway. "What's the matter with you?"

"Nothing. What're you talking about?"

"You've been acting weird."

"I might be coming down with something," I say, giving a small cough for added effect.

A cough isn't something to be taken lightly, and she backs away slightly, just in case. But she continues to pester. "I know why we've had so many visitors lately." Her voice is smug and I can tell she's bursting to share her secret.

"Okay. Why?"

"We're being tagged."

"What?"

She nods her head sagely. "All the girls in the orphanage. It's a new policy for population management. We're having microchips embedded. So the Territory Council can keep track, I guess."

I can't believe it. Chips are for prisoners, the

occasional captured felon who at some point hacked into a Council computer or tried to steal more than his ration of water. Chips aren't for kids.

"Orphans don't get chips," I whisper.

"They do now. I overheard Matron talking." She tugs on my sleeve, breaking through my growing unease.

"What?" My voice is impatient, I know, but I want to be alone with my thoughts. I want to think about what the traveler said, and now there's this crazy microchip business. What does it mean?

"There's no water in your dish," says Mary. "I checked under your bed. Did you water the flower today?"

I glance around, grabbing her arm to pull her closer. "Hush, Mary. Someone will hear you."

"No one's listening."

"Does the flower look like it needs water?"

"Well," her face registers momentary confusion. "No."

"Fine. Then I'm doing my part. Stop bothering me."

She yanks her arm back, her face flushed. "I was asking to be thoughtful, Kira. In the future, I won't waste my time." She stomps off, leaving me with a vague feeling of shame. For the first time in my life, I have someone who's being nice to me and, even though I'm inexperienced at this friendship business, I know I'm not keeping up my end of things.

Quickly, I gather my cushion and head out to the shed. Even in the fading light of dusk, I can tell the flower looks great. If possible, it looks fresher than when it was a new bloom. Whatever's happening, it must be a good thing, I decide. Otherwise, why would the flower be doing so well? I'm being a worrywart.

I lean forward, resting my arms on the pillow. I'm tired and confused, and I hate this feeling that things are going on around me I can't control. I need to think things through and this is my best spot for thinking. First, however, I need to take care of something.

"I wish for water," I say softly, keeping my eyes on the flower, waiting for the familiar dark stain to make its way across the dirt.

Hearing the rattle of pebbles followed by a quiet gasp, I snap my head up and see Mary. She's gazing at the ground in horror, her eyes round as she watches the water now forming a puddle around the slender green stem.

"Mary, let me explain," I stammer, hopping up. Of course, there's no explanation for this, and we both know it.

She backs away, her eyes darting between me and the damp ground. Abruptly, she turns and runs to the house.

I'm frozen in place, dismayed that I've been caught and embarrassed to have my ability—or freakish disability—known by anyone. Then I remember the flower. Mary's going to give it away. Shoot! Shoot! Shoot! I have to catch her. I have to get her back on my side before she ruins everything.

I move now, dashing after Mary. But my pause cost me. Halfway back to the house, I encounter Matron, followed by Mary and the other girls. Matron's face is purple, her expression one of unqualified rage. Panic-stricken at this turn of events, I pivot, ready to dart away, but Matron grabs hold of my shoulder and pushes me toward the back of the shed.

I hear Mary's sniffles behind me and shoot her a dark look. That crybaby. Why did I ever think she was my friend? She cowers behind Matron, gawking at me as if I were something evil.

When Matron reaches the back of the shed, she lets out a low growl, her grip on me tightening. What is it about a flower that would make a person so angry, I wonder.

Pinning me with a furious gaze, she points toward the flower. "Yank it," she says tersely.

My jaw drops and I shake my head slowly. "I will not," I whisper, horrified

"It's illegal. It doesn't belong here. Either you re-move it, or I will."

I continue to shake my head, blinking back tears. I'm vaguely aware that I'm trembling, but it's like some-thing outside myself, totally unconnected to me. Vainly, I press my hands against my stomach and the anguish beginning to seize there.

Matron moves forward and grabs the flower by the base of the stem. With one savage tug, she rips it out of the ground, damp soil clinging to the roots. A small squeak behind me has her turning a heated gaze to Mary. "Brace up, girl," she barks. "It's only a flower."

"It's only a flower," I repeat softly, dully, but I can feel my mind rebelling. It was more. It was beauty and it was life and for me, for a short while, it had been a thing of joy and purpose.

5

Grounded!

I hurl my book at the closed door, followed by a shoe and a hairbrush. No one responds to my fury. I'm alone in the room, forbidden to step outside the door.

Of course, Mary blabbed everything. Matron focused on the criminal presence of the flower, attributing the rest of Mary's hysteria to adolescent melodrama and stress brought on by my bad influence. After all, Matron said, the truth of my transgression was bad enough without Mary adding a bunch of hogwash about me being able to conjure water. And yet…and yet, Matron had sent me the strangest look. For just a moment, it felt like she was afraid of me.

Nah.

Throwing myself back onto the bed, I plot how to get even with Mary Castle. I begin with simple tortures, a lizard in her underwear drawer or a well-timed rumor to discredit her among the other girls. I should never have let her near me or my flower. My flower. Gone now. My breath hitches and I can feel the anger slipping away. I reel it back. I need my anger. I need it to keep away the other stuff.

Slowly, a new worry grabs hold of me. Matron had promised that after one more infraction, she'd send me away. Would she? My stomach churns and I press my hand against my belly, willing what's there to stay there. I force myself to breathe slowly, and it passes. So what if she does send me away? I give the bed a good kick. It's not like the Garner Home for Girls has been doing me any favors lately.

Suddenly, an idea pops into my head. It's so outrageous that at first I can't get my mind around it. It's too huge. But what if—I feel a shiver of anticipation—what if I left on my own? That would show them. Matron would learn that she doesn't have power over me. I don't need them. I don't need anybody.

I stand and start to pace. The traveler who'd shared his stories, he'd traveled everywhere. It wasn't impossible. But, where would I go? How would I survive?

I can make my own water, of course. That's something. Whoa! I halt mid-step, suddenly light-headed. *I can make my own water*. The ramifications of this slowly sink into place. I can *do* something. I can do something huge, something that will impress everybody. Watering my flower, that mattered, but it mattered only to me. What if I did something that mattered to others, to a lot of others, in fact? What if I could make more than just a puddle?

Desperate to reassure myself I can do this thing, I run to a cupboard and pull out a cup. I pull it close and wish for water. Nothing happens. I drop the cup with a clatter and kneel on the floor.

"I want water," I whisper. Nothing happens. "I wish for it," I say, my voice breaking. "I wish for water." Not a drop appears on the hard floor.

"Okay." I try to calm myself. "This doesn't mean a thing. So what if I can't make water fill a cup? And why in the world would water appear on the bedroom floor? That's ridiculous. It's illogical. Clearly, I have to wish for water with a purpose, or I have to wish for water in its natural environment. That's all."

I'm not reassured.

I don't give myself time to back out. I know myself well enough to understand that if I think about my plan for too long, I'll find a way to talk myself out of it.

When the other girls come into the room, I feel their glances and ignore their soft whispers. I curl in bed, my eyes closed tightly. I've used the time alone to pack my backpack with the essentials: a small bedroll, a change of clothes and a hat, my nutritionals, a first aid kit, a flashlight and enough sun block to get me through, I think. My backpack will hold my entire life inside it. From this point on, I can't let it out of my sight.

Hopefully, I don't need to worry about water, but food's a concern. Of course, bugs will be plentiful. Aside from algae, bugs make up our primary source of protein at the orphanage. Thinking of Cook's famous stir-fry of white beetles with rock salt and sage, I salivate. Cook has a gift in the kitchen. Whether it's grubs or crickets, she knows how to turn out a tasty meal. Feeling a pang in my stomach, I push the thought away. I can't think of that now. I have to learn to rough it and eat my mealworms raw.

After the other girls are asleep, I tiptoe to the kitchen. Very gently, I pull a step ladder over to the wall. Climbing to the highest cabinet, I take a small hammer stolen from the tool box and break the lock on one of the doors. Inside is a lithium ion global positioning device, one of Matron's most cherished possessions. I can't resist a smile at the thought of her expression when she realizes it's gone. I close the cabinet and return the step ladder to its proper place. Finally, I fill my backpack with trail mix and algae bars. I am quiet. It is dark. No one hears me leave.

I walk quickly, not looking back. This instant in time feels momentous, weighted with importance, and I know I'll remember it for the rest of my life. I'm scared, trembling so hard it's a wonder I can stand, but I force myself to take step after step. If I only take one step at a time, I can do this thing. As long as I don't think too much about tomorrow or next week or the week after, I can make myself move forward. With conscious thought, I remind myself to breathe.

I'm afraid to be out in the dark. I'm afraid to be alone. But I'm more afraid to stop moving or to glance back, to lose the momentum of my outrageous idea. I'll walk until I find a place to hide during the hottest part of the day. That's when I'll sleep.

There's just enough moon to light my way, but with my vision diminished by darkness, my other senses reach out, searching around me. There are odors in the dark—thick and musky, but tinged with something bitter and metallic I can taste on my tongue.

My mother's photo is in my pocket, and I press my hand against it for comfort. Delta Territory is far, but it's where I'm determined to go, to make water and, maybe, to find answers.

Glancing at the illuminated GPS, I change direction slightly and continue heading north. At first, I notice everything: the air, the stars; the hum of generators when I pass some habitation. After awhile, however, I grow bored with my surroundings, the flat, dark plainness of it. I play mental games to keep myself awake and moving. I try to think of all the wet words in the English language, words that disappeared from use along with the water. You can still find the wet words in old books, words like *drenched, saturated, soaking, soggy, sodden* and *swamped*. Great, thick, rich words.

By midnight, my word games have ended, and I'm nearly in tears. My feet hurt. The muscles in my legs ache and pull with every step. If I had to get some crazy ability, why couldn't it be the ability to fly? I wonder, briefly, if there's someone, somewhere, who has that ability. If there is, I wonder if she's stumbled upon her strange talent. Perhaps, mid-fall, she suddenly spread her arms and took flight. Or maybe she'll never spread her arms and the ability will lie quiet, undiscovered, her entire life.

31

Suddenly, I stop. What if *I* can fly? What if there are other things I can wish for that I haven't thought to try? What if my wish for water was just the first of three wishes, or six or ten? I think for a minute then hold out my hands, palms up. "I wish for food to fill my hands."

Nothing happens.

Maybe I need to be more specific. "I wish for a handful of nuts," I say loudly. "I wish for roasted hemp nuts." I lift my hands into the air, ready to have them filled.

Nothing happens.

I drop my hands and glance up into the night sky.

"I wish it would rain."

Nothing.

"I wish I could fly."

I give a small hop into the air, arms outstretched, and when I land, my right calf cramps, sending a wave of pain shooting up my leg.

"Drat!" Feeling foolish, I massage my leg until the muscle relaxes. Evidently, I've got one wish that works. I guess that's more than most. Taking a deep breath, I force myself forward. Soon, I can rest.

I eat a handful of trail mix just before morning, then sneak into a shed behind a wind farm to hide out. It's too dangerous to be out in the sunlight mid-day. Boxes and tools line the wall of the shed, and I sneak into a crowded corner, drop my backpack onto the floor, and lay my head against the cool nylon. The wind turbines make a swishing noise I find soothing, and I sleep.

I spend day after day like this, walking north with the moonlight, then finding a place to hide before the sun comes out. Sore legs and swollen feet give way to firm calves and a steady heart. I'm the fittest that I've ever been in my life.

I'm also the loneliest.

6

When I emerge from my hiding place each evening, the sun is waning, shadows stretching across the salt pan until the heavy collapse of the night swallows me up and the land with it. I find beauty in the darkness and laugh at myself for it. I know I'm being sappy.

Early one evening, as I'm bypassing an abandoned town—a relic of empty buildings and crumbled concrete—I turn a corner and there's a creek. The creek is black and covered in patches of orange toxic froth. The closer I come to the foamy fluid, the harder it is to breathe. I hold my nose as I pass, shivering at this noxious stuff that passes for water.

Anxious to get away from the fumes, I stride purposefully, my mind on the trek ahead of me; my eyes, evidently, elsewhere. I trip, falling forward over an obstacle in my path, and hold out my hands to catch myself. "Oof...*oww!*"

"What the...!"

"Hey!"

"Get off!"

I roll sideways, stunned by the appearance of a boy.

"Why don'tcha watch where you're going?" he snaps.

"What were you doing? Sleeping in the middle of the path?"

"I wasn't sleeping," he says, grumpily. "And this isn't a path."

My eyes follow the cleared space into the distance. "It *is* a path." I pause, frowning at the untidy person before me. "What are you doing?"

"Studyin' something."

He stretches back out on the ground, pulling his head and shoulders onto the path again—it *is* a path—and I can't help but admire the look of him. He's attractive in a lanky, loose-jointed sort of way. He has sandy brown hair, and I notice immediately his striking eyes, not the washed-out blue of the sky, but a blue that's bright and penetrating.

I'm not imagining things. It's a boy. And not like the weathered travelers who would appear at the orphanage hoping for a handout, but someone my own age. The last time I saw a boy my age was when the Garner Home invited the nearest boys' home to attend a day-long training session on the vegetation drought response index.

I crouch down to see what he's doing and wince, suddenly aware that my palms are scraped and bleeding. Toxic soil in an open wound can be deadly. Thank goodness I received a tetanus shot last year. And, I've got antiseptic in my pack. Gingerly this time, I inch toward the ground, my eyes following his to...what?

"What is it?" I whisper.

"It's a toad, you idiot."

I don't see why he has to be snippy. I can see it's a toad, but like no toad I've ever encountered before. It's a mature deviant.

The creature in question is hopping, sort of, but is unable to travel in a straight line. It moves sideways, topples over, rights itself, then hops sideways again, and falls.

The toad has five legs and two of the legs jut out the side of his body, not beneath, like the others. It's impossible for him to hop properly.

The deviants are the plants and animals—often babies—that have been twisted by toxins in the air and soil and water, and in the microscopic cells of mothers everywhere. From birth, they're penalized. Most die early. A few survive.

"What should we do?" I ask, looking to this boy for an answer. "Should we put it out of its misery?"

"Maybe we should put *you* out of *your* misery," he responds hotly.

I sit back on my heels, caught off guard by his hostility. What does he mean? Is he implying...? But how could he...?

Abruptly, he stands. "What'd this toad ever do to you?" Picking up the unbalanced creature, he moves it carefully into an area thick with dead, tangled vines. I watch him carefully, trying to decide what to do. I don't know much about boys, and I'm curious to see what he'll do next. He seems harmless enough. Once he's satisfied the toad is in a protected spot, he turns back.

"My name's Kira," I say, sticking out my hand. I want to be nice. This boy's prickly, but he's the first person my age I've seen in a long time. Suddenly, I snatch my hand back, realizing that in order to shake it, he must touch it with the hand that only seconds earlier held the toad.

He looks at me with a disdain that makes me feel small inside.

"It's not contagious," he says, his voice soft.

I flush angrily. "I know that."

A silent pause stretches between us. Our gazes are assessing, cautious.

"I'm J.D.," he says finally. He reaches behind a pile of rocks and pulls out a backpack. "You can walk with me a ways if you want."

"Um...okay."

Silently, I fall into place beside him, watching him out of the corner of my eye. I like the way he moves, easily, slender hips pulling the rest of him forward.

"Where're you headed?" he asks.

"Delta Territory."

His eyes widen, darting to mine. "The Dead Lakes Region?"

"To Slag."

He stumbles, catching himself before he hits the ground. "Why in the world would you go there? It's nothing but a ghost town."

I shrug. Everyone knows Slag's uninhabitable. Of course, it wasn't always a desolate place, and it wasn't always called Slag. Once upon a time, the city had a lovely name and houses with kids playing in front yards. Years of industrial development along the shores of the Lakes Region eventually gave way to a completely toxic environment. Then the city was hit hard by the Devastation, chemical and biological warfare that spread across continents and still created casualties years after the surrender, as chemicals and enzymes mixed with other substances and evolved into something unforeseen.

"What about you?" I ask.

"I go where the wind takes me," he says, lifting one bony shoulder.

I lick my finger and stick it high into the air, testing. "What wind?"

He scowls.

"Just kidding," I say quickly. I don't know this boy well enough to make jokes at his expense. He's the first person I've had to talk with in days. The last thing I want is to offend him.

"Do you have family?" I ask.

"Nope."

"Me neither." I fiddle with the strap of my backpack. "What does 'J.D.' stand for?"

"Just Deserts," he says shortly. "As in 'some day, I will get my just deserts.'"

I stare at him blankly. His expression gives nothing away.

"I don't believe you," I say finally. "Besides, are you so sure that getting your *just desserts* will be a good thing?"

He doesn't answer and we walk for a moment in silence.

"So how long have you been traveling?" I ask.

He shoots me a glance, but doesn't slow down. "I don't really like chit chat."

"Oh. Yeah. Me neither."

For a while, I hum softly under my breath. I'm feeling delighted with myself, to have found someone to keep me company, even for a little while. "I've got trail mix in my pack, and algae bars—if you get hungry later, I mean."

I don't tell him I've learned to steal, raiding the larders of lonely outposts or sneaking into empty kitchens after dark. I figure if he's been out walking very long, he's developed his own nimble fingers. At least I try to repay my burglaries by leaving behind a small pond or a suddenly full gully.

J.D. eyes me, then my backpack, his expression a little too uninterested to be believed. "Sure."

I smile and forge ahead. I'm halfway there.

7

I don't know what J.D. had in mind when he said I could travel with him "a ways," but a week later, we're still walking. And he's still a stranger to me. His demeanor doesn't invite questions, and he tends to ignore the ones I do ask. On the other hand, he hasn't asked me to get lost either.

He carries a water filter in his backpack and uses it to filter the brackish water of private algae ponds. First, he tests the ponds, pulling up a small sample in order to measure microcystin levels. Even with testing and use of the filter, which is supposed to screen out over ten different types of water-borne diseases, sometimes he gets sick, shaking with nausea and fever. He says he used to have tablets, micocystin antibodies and mixing powders that would clump together the pollution and parasites for easier filtering, but he's run out.

Once, when there's no algae pond available, I watch him fill both our bottles with murky water from a standpipe. Then he places the filled bottles on a piece of metal in full sunlight. By the time we wake up, seven hours later, UVA radiation has killed any viruses, bacteria and

40

parasites in the water, making it safe to drink.

His methods are uncertain and time-consuming and I especially don't like it when he's sick, so I develop the habit of "discovering" water once we've halted in the morning or at twilight when we're ready to set out for the next stage of our trek. Usually, once we find a shelter to hide out during the day, I make it my job to scout the surroundings. I can almost always find a small depression to fill and, while the water level's rising, I scrounge around for edible insects.

It's J.D.'s job to set up camp and start a small fire, if it seems safe. When I show up with water, I tell him it's from an abandoned well or an industrial tank. He always tests the water first, before taking a sip. He's very careful. The water I make is good, and he doesn't get sick from drinking it.

Early one evening I'm feeling pretty proud of my successful subterfuge when he catches me in the act. I glance across the small ditch I've just filled to see him standing at the edge of the clearing, a look of bewilderment on his face.

"How'd you do that?"

I watch him cautiously. He hasn't taken his eyes off the water, like he's afraid it will disappear if he blinks.

"I don't know."

He turns his gaze to me. "Do it again."

I stand, dusting off my jeans. Realizing my expression might give me away, I turn my face. "It's not a party trick," I say shortly. I'm scared. It's not like J.D. is great company, but he's some company and, for a few days, it was nice not to be alone. I can't remember a time in my life when I didn't feel lonely, whether I was truly alone or not. But I don't feel alone when I'm with J.D. Only, now he's sure to leave. And I'll go back to walking alone, talking to myself and being alone in the dark. I cap my water bottle and head toward the campsite.

"I wondered why you never seemed concerned with conserving water," he says slowly, jogging to keep up. "I remember thinking you were like one of those camels I've read about, hiding a couple of humps somewhere."

I say nothing. What is there to say? At least a camel would be something natural, something along the normal order of things.

"Hey, what's the matter with you? You have this thing, this—well, it's amazing when you think about it," he says. I keep walking, daunted by the words pouring out of his mouth. He hasn't said this much in an entire week. "You should be doing something with this, you know. You should be conjuring water for a living. I bet you'd get paid loads for a thing like this. You waltz into a place, fill up the local reservoir, pick up a stash of credits and live like a king...I mean, queen."

I bend over to refold my bedroll, then turn to tie it to my pack. J.D. grabs my shoulder and when I feel his touch, it's too much. I spin around, slapping his hand away.

"Back off!" My hands are clenched so tightly the knuckles form a white ridge that mirrors our horizon. "Do you think I don't know all that? Sure, it'd be nice to help people. I want to eat a real meal and sleep in a real bed. But, I don't know why I have this ability. I don't know where it comes from or what it means. I'm a freak, J.D., just like that five-legged frog of yours."

"Toad."

"Whatever." I take a bitter breath and let it out. "I don't want to be turned into some sideshow attraction. I don't want to draw attention to myself. And I especially don't want anyone telling me what to do!"

Instantly, his face shuts down. I push away my sudden feeling of remorse. Geez Louise. Part of me wants to recall my words and stuff them back into my mouth, but it's too late. And I won't let him see me being weak.

"Fine," he says shortly. He turns to pack up his stuff. "Hey, it's your thing. You can do whatever you want with it or nothing at all. It's no skin off my nose."

"Teeth."

"What?"

"It's no skin off my teeth," I say tiredly. "That's the expression."

He frowns then shakes his head. "Teeth don't have skin," he mutters.

I nibble my lip, considering. "You're right. Your way makes more sense."

We finish our packing in silence and set off, our eyes on the landscape ahead of us. We're in the foothills now, heading toward a Biosphere. I've always avoided the larger communities, but J.D. wants to stock up on supplies. He says he knows somebody who can get us more sun block, the really good stuff. Now that the weather's cooling down, it would be nice to do our walking during

43

the day and our sleeping at night.

For the last week, I've traveled with J.D. in a comfortable silence. Suddenly, the silence is so brittle it crackles. I wish he hadn't seen me make water. And I wish I hadn't snapped at him. For once, he was actually, I don't know, animated. He was talking to me. And I want to trust him. I wonder if he knows I watch him sometimes when he's not looking. It makes me happy to watch him. But it makes me feel foolish, too. And the truth is I really don't know him. What if he tells someone my secret? Especially if he thinks my ability to make water is something to be traded for credits. It could totally wreck my plans.

Of course, a part of me thinks J.D. has the right idea. Why not sell my talent for a few credits? Is it the fear of unknown consequences that holds me back? Or maybe it's the memory of that look in Mary's eyes when she caught me making water, the look that marks me as distinctly *other*. Maybe that's it. If my ability becomes common knowledge then I'll never be able to, I don't know, belong...anywhere.

It's late when we come across a fantastic looking tree illuminated by silvery moonlight. One side of the tree has been damaged, leaving the other half lopsided and twisted. Misshapen branches reach out and up and a small area close to the tree trunk bears clusters of leaves. The leaves are green. Even at night, there's no mistaking it.

We stop in our tracks, stunned by this sign of life. It's probably a fluke, some strange coinciding of just the right timing and conditions, but it is life straight out of barrenness, and I feel hopeful.

Hopeful, but cautious. After all, I've been trudging over bare, baked earth for days. And now my secret's out. I glance at J.D. and wonder if I should leave him once we've gotten to the Biosphere and I've had a chance to restock my pack. Maybe it's time.

"The moon's bright tonight," he says abruptly. "We could walk a little further."

I drop my backpack onto the ground beneath the tree and its surprising sign of life. "I'm tired." I stretch out my bedroll and plop down. "I want to cut it short tonight."

I wait, expecting an argument, half expecting him to wave good-bye and keep walking without me. Finally, his pack drops, and I silently release the breath I've been holding.

I look up to see him gazing at the moon and take the moment to examine him unobserved. He has a nice profile. I follow his gaze. It *is* a bright moon, round and incandescent.

"I see the man in the moon," I say softly, turning over and tucking my hands beneath my head.

"He looks like he's singing."

"The moon was bigger last night. Did you notice?"

"The moon's always the same size."

"Fine, it wasn't bigger, but it *looked* bigger."

He sighs, giving up, and spreads out his bedroll to sleep. Of course, I know that the moon, the moon that orbits the planet and has scientific qualities, I know

45

that moon possesses a constant size and shape. But the moon I see, the one that faces me now in the dark of night, this moon is full of mysterious changes. Tonight, it's big and oddly reassuring. The man in the moon smiles at me. I'm unable to smile back.

Nervously, I clear my throat. "J.D.?"

"Hmm?"

"I...um...I want to...apologize."

"What?"

I hear him turn over and face me, but I continue to stare up at the night sky.

"I don't know much about boys."

"What's that got to do with anything?"

"I don't know. I just...."

"You don't know much. Period."

Stung, I whip my head around. "Hey, I know things."

His lips twitch, and I can't tell if he's smiling. He better not be smiling.

"I wasn't trying to tell you what to do," he says quietly.

"Oh." I wait to see if there's more.

"So what *are* you going to do?"

I scratch my nose and give a small shrug. "Go to Slag."

"You probably don't want to go all that way by yourself."

I purse my lips thoughtfully, imagining the distance I still have to travel. "Well, no, you're probably right."

"Your chances of making it will be better if you're not alone," he says.

"Yes."

"Okay then."

8

The next day, we arrive at Bio-4, one of a dozen domed cities in the territory. It isn't fully enclosed, but it's protected from harsh ultra-violet rays by a huge geodesic cover. Fields of soybeans, hydrated through drip irrigation, stretch outside the perimeter, while more delicate vegetation is nurtured inside the dome.

J.D. and I get onto the north-south road and enter with other travelers. It's cool inside and dim, like the underground cities. It's good to see so many people moving around above ground, without fear of the sun. It feels friendly.

I hear the sound of running feet and glance across the road. An artist with a strong sense of the fantastic has painted a life-size *trompe l'oeil* mural on an outside wall. Beautifully-rendered splashing fountains send a white spray of water into the sky. As I watch, a small child runs up and presses her tongue to the wall, then steps back in confusion and disappointment.

J.D. and I exchange a glance. He grabs my elbow and steers me away. "Come on," he says.

We walk into the interior, taking in all the activity

around us. I try to absorb the sounds and smells of the noisy, crowded market. It's disconcerting to be among people again. There are stalls of food, real food, not the pressed, packaged stuff. There are baskets of kelp, as well as squash and beans and chili peppers. My eyes nearly fall out of my head when I see apples. I can't remember the last time I tasted an apple, but my mouth is watering at the sight of it, and I tug on J.D. to get his attention.

"I want one of those apples."

"There are too many people around," he whispers into my ear. "Right now, just keep your eyes open."

My eyes, however, aren't the only thing being assaulted. All of my senses are on alert and now it's my nose that causes me to stop in my tracks. A sidewalk vendor is selling roasted crickets and the smell has me salivating, holding onto my stomach with both hands. I'm so hungry. J.D. senses my torment and steers me down a side street, away from the food and the distraction it causes.

Bio-4 contains several wide foam-biotic lots around the inside perimeter where travelers can bed down temporarily, sheltered by the dome. Numbered parking spaces are available for rent. After giving the superintendent a credit (I don't ask where he got it), J.D. and I are assigned space sixty-eight.

We snake through the crowd of people and find our space, eight by ten square feet of insulated surface made from organic materials. We drop our packs and turn to check out our neighbor. Lot sixty-seven contains two occupants, a dark young woman with a baby on her lap.

"Hello," we say, cautiously.

"Hello."

J.D. steps forward. "I'm J.D., and this is Kira."

"It's nice to meet you. My name is Tamara. This is my daughter, Shay."

I step closer to shake Tamara's hand. She's sitting on a small stool, the baby in her lap. J.D. kneels down to get a better view of the baby and becomes fixated, gazing with fascination into wide, staring eyes. The baby girl, Shay, looks like a small Buddha, her serene face crowned with dark curls.

J.D. and the baby gaze at each other, engaged in a spontaneous staring match. The baby doesn't know she's a competitor in the contest. Nevertheless, she wins. J.D. blinks, and the baby turns her wide, curious eyes to me.

"How old is she?" I ask the mother, stroking the baby's large round head.

"Eight months."

I love the silky feel of her curls. They remind me of the softness of my flower back at the orphanage, filling me with a sudden and unexpected sense of loss. My fingers tuck a curl behind the baby's ear and I freeze at the sight of a second, half-developed ear just below it. I glance to the other side of her head where loose curls cover whatever ear or ears are there.

Gently, the mother untucks the hair, letting it fall back into place, concealing the tiny deformity.

Both J.D. and the mother are watching me. The baby, of course, has not blinked. I can feel their questioning expressions, even though I don't look up. I know they're waiting for my reaction. I'm jarred by what I've seen. I can't deny it. But clearly, this child is sweet and endearing. I wonder if she has great hearing.

I raise my eyes to catch the mother's gaze on me. Her eyes are wary, as if daring me to slight her child in some way.

"She's adorable," I say softly.

"Thank you."

We chat for another moment then J.D. and I move to our pad and sit to discuss our next steps.

"I'm going to find Tuck and get us more sun block."

"We're out of food, J.D. I think that should be our first priority." My stomach's growling and I'm unable to think about anything else. "We're sheltered by the dome now. The sun block can wait. I want to eat."

"It takes credits to eat in the Biosphere, Kira. Tuck may be able to help me with that, too. Just promise you won't steal anything. There are too many people around. You'll get caught."

"I beg your pardon? I've managed not to get caught so far. I don't know why it'd be any different in the Biosphere."

"Trust me. It's different. For one thing, there are cameras everywhere, even places you can't see them. For another thing, territory officials patrol the streets, especially in the marketplace. Don't even think about getting away with anything here."

"Then what am I suppose to do?" Why am I even asking him? J.D. is not the boss of me. I don't need his permission to do anything.

"Just sit tight for now. I'm going to see if Tuck can set me up in a temporary job. With a few credits in my pocket, we can restock our supplies."

We do need to restock, that's true. Bugs provide ample protein, as well as calcium and iron. But it's a balanced mixture of red, green and brown algae that supplies our vitamins and minerals, as well as important fatty acids. Without algae bars, our energy levels will be too low to keep walking. And I want an apple.

"See if your friend can get me a job, too," I say suddenly, surprising myself.

He stares at me curiously. "What do you know how to do?"

I don't say 'make water,' because it's obvious I can't do that here. There's nothing else, really, I know how to do.

"I'm smart. I can learn to do anything."

"We're not going to be here long enough for you to learn a trade, Kira. I need to know what you're willing to do right now to earn credits."

"I can clean house," I snap. "I'm not afraid to get down on my hands and knees and scrub. And I could babysit for someone."

"Then that's what I'll try and find." He stands and looks down at me. "I don't know how long this will take. Are you going to be okay here by yourself?"

I don't say a word, just cross my arms and give him a look. He grabs his pack and leaves without another word.

I watch him slip out of the parking lot, his thin frame disappearing into the crowd. Why did I do that? Okay, sure, I hate being treated like a baby, and I really, really hate anybody telling me what to do. But maybe he was trying to be thoughtful. After all, he knows more than I do about being in a Biosphere. He was probably being nice, and I responded by being a jerk. Way to go, Kira. I want to kick myself. Then just as suddenly, I'm angry with myself for being angry with myself, which makes no sense at all. I drop my head into my hands. Why is being around other people so hard?

I mope for a while, chin in my hands, watching the other travelers in the lot. There are both families and solitary drifters spread out on their patch of rented space, pushing bedrolls and possessions up to the limit of their boundaries. I watch them going about their small, daily tasks until, finally, I can't sit still a moment longer.

There's simply no reason why I can't explore on my own. It's not like I have to sit here and guard our space. J.D. paid for it. And according to him, there are security cameras and personnel monitoring every square inch of the camping lot.

I jump up, slip my pack over my shoulder and head east along a wide boulevard. It's overwhelming to be part of a crowd all of a sudden. But it's invigorating, too. I laugh out loud, for no reason at all. I watch people bartering at food stands, workers climbing enormous scaffolds to repair holes in the dome, and kids playing hopscotch on the sidewalks.

I enter a particularly dense area, drinking in the sounds and smells. Market stalls crowd together, filled with household goods, handcrafted sandals and men hawking the latest cure-all for whatever's ailing a person. As I pass a small shop, a woman reaches out and grabs my arm. I inhale a rich, musky odor and glance into the wrinkled face of a woman with wide, white eyes.

"Let me tell your fortune," she whispers.

I hang back, reluctant to enter the gloomy doorway looming behind her. One swift tug would free my arm from the woman's grasp, but it would also drag her right off her feet. She's tiny, looks to be half my weight, and I've grown strong during my journey.

"Let me tell your fortune," she repeats.

"I don't have any credits."

"Let me tell your fortune."

Giving in, I let her lead me through the dark doorway into a room filled with shadows. A small lamp illuminates her table, a stack of crates covered in hemp cloth. She motions me to a stool, and I sit.

She grabs my hand and pulls it toward her. She runs her fingers over my palm and I can't tell if she's actually seeing something there or not. Her white eyes have me spooked. I'm not sure if they're contacts, masking the true nature of her pupils, or maybe she's blind. If she's blind then surely she can't read my palm, she can only *feel* it. Finally she speaks, her voice low and hoarse.

"'In the world there is nothing more submissive and weak than water. Yet for attacking that which is hard and strong, nothing can surpass it.' Loud Zoo said that."

53

What in the world? I look into the woman's milky eyes, trying to figure this out. "Loud who?"

She drops my hand. "You may go."

I stare at my hand, limp on the table, as though it's something apart from me. Then I glare at the old woman. "That's it? That's all you have to say?"

"Be careful." She stands and leaves the room, her long skirt swishing softly as she heads into the dark recesses of her shop.

"What?" I stare after her retreating back, feeling alternately baffled, then angry. How dare she drag me in here promising me a reading, only to deliver some stupid, cryptic quotation—no matter that I didn't want my fortune told in the first place. "Well, *that* was a cracked fortune," I shout into the darkness, finally finding my voice. "I hope you do a better job with the people who actually *pay* to hear what you have to say."

9

"I know everything there is to know about Bio-4," says the man called Tuck. "I know the guys with the goods and the guys who want 'em. I take a shipment of hemp oil off the grid and deliver it to the guys who have the microprocessor chips. For chips, I can make a fair exchange of black market tobacco and get crates of pilfered sun block and nutritionals."

I hurry to keep up with him. His stride is short and quick. He speeds ahead of me like an automated toy, talking as fast as he moves. I've never met anyone like this pale character. He's simultaneously savvy and childlike.

"Where's J.D.?" I ask.

"He's speaking with friends of mine," Tuck says, grabbing my arm and steering me around a crowded corner. "He's going to work at the local algae operation, testing and cleaning, stuff like that."

"Oh."

"I told him I'd fetch ya from the lot and take you over to this factory I know. They're always looking for people. Nuthin' fancy, but it's steady work."

"Um…Okay."

"Don't worry. They won't inquire too much into yer background."

I hadn't worried about it at all actually, but when he mentions it, I realize how awkward it would be if people started asking for papers or personal information.

"How do you know J.D.?" I ask.

"Oh we go way back. We used to get into trouble together back in Gamma."

"I never knew J.D. lived in Gamma Territory." The truth is, I still don't know much about J.D. at all. He's never shared much about himself, so naturally, I'm consumed with curiosity.

"Sure. Me and him been all over. We were locked up together for awhile back east."

"Locked up for what?"

He slips me a sideways glance. "Oh, for takin' shortcuts," he says vaguely. He stops in front of a bleak-looking building near the edge of the dome and gestures toward the door. "This is it. Hemp processing. I toldcha it weren't fancy. But, it'll put credits in your pocket while yer here."

"Don't you need to come in with me?"

"Nah. They're expectin' ya."

I glance at him in alarm. "How am I going to find my way back to the camping lot?"

"Oh, that's easy," he says, grinning. "I know this whole place like the back a' my hand. When you come out, you'll want to go down this street right here." He gestures down the road we've just traveled. "Three blocks down then three blocks to the right to the solar power station. Through the tunnel then two blocks straight ahead and yer there."

I nod dumbly, repeating the words in my head. With a wave and a wink, he's gone.

Sure enough, the minute I walk in, I'm put to work, no questions asked. After weeks spent outdoors, being indoors is dreary and suffocating. I keep to myself, as do the other workers. The conditions in the plant are blatantly sub-standard, which is no doubt why I'm able to get work here in the first place. There's inadequate ventilation and the air is full of throat-clogging dust. Mounds of hemp debris create a fire hazard, not to mention the physical strain we endure, standing at spinning machines or working in the pulping room. My employers are in violation of a dozen different health and safety codes. No one appears to care.

When the workday is over, I'm haggard and dehydrated. I stumble back the way Tuck brought me, losing my way once. Weaving through the thick traffic of people making their way to homes or encampments, I spot J.D. ahead in the crowd and give a tired wave. With the sleeve of my shirt, I wipe sweat from my face, shoving back tendrils of hair stuck to my skin.

"Here. This is for you."

I drop my arm, curious to see what he's got. J.D. grabs my hand and pulls it toward him, placing a small apple in the center of my palm.

Oh. My. This is the first time anyone has ever given me a gift. I keep my head down, blinking at the apple.

"What's wrong?" he asks.

"Nothing's wrong." I force my eyes wide, willing them dry. "Want to share it with me?"

"I was hoping you'd ask."

He takes the apple and with his pocketknife cuts it in half, handing me my piece.

And it is good.

So begins a strange, new daily existence. J.D. and I work at our jobs. It is hard, mindless labor. Perhaps hard because it is so mindless. But when the work is done, we meet back at lot sixty-eight and, along with Tamara and Baby Shay who have spent their day selling handcrafted jewelry in the marketplace, we set off to explore Bio-4, searching among the sidewalk vendors for what we want to eat each evening. With credits in our pockets, we purchase fresh kelp and roasted beetles in hot sauce. For dessert, J.D. and I split an apple. Always, I'm reluctant to let even a little of the juice dribble down my chin and lap up the wayward sweetness with my tongue.

The days blend one into another as we get comfortable in our new environment. Occasionally, I feel guilty for not being on the road, heading north like I'd planned, but it's nice here, in spite of my crummy job. Tamara is a friend and I can no longer imagine waking up without the soft tugs and coos of Baby Shay.

I think J.D. likes it here, too. He appears more relaxed. He still doesn't say much, but he seems to enjoy a sense of accomplishment from tasks completed, dividing his time between the outdoor ponds and indoor labs. Neither one of us speaks of leaving, although the topic frequently hangs unspoken in the air between us.

Today, we meet after work and discover Tamara has brought us a treat.

"I exchanged a pair of earrings for tickets to a movie," she says excitedly.

I glance at the ticket she hands me and read the title out loud. "*Circus Adventure.*" I give her a quizzical glance. This is something new. "What's a circus?"

"I'm not sure. But the girl who gave me these said it was entertainment."

I glance at J.D., and he shrugs. I've never seen entertainment, but I'm willing to give it a try. After grabbing a quick bite to eat, the three of us with Baby Shay follow directions to a small auditorium tucked behind the power station. It's dark inside when we take our seats, and there's an air of expectancy in the room. I've seen movies before, of course. At the Garner Home, we watched movies about the proper way to irrigate and how to construct a home recycling station. We saw historical footage of battles and natural catastrophes. But I've never watched a movie this way before, with a dark room full of strangers seeking entertainment. So when tinkly music fills the room, I inch forward in my seat along with the others. And watch a movie about the circus.

When it's over, we exit quietly from the building.

"I don't understand." I frown, trying to make sense

59

of the images I saw on the big screen. I feel sad, even though it was clear in the movie that the circus was intended to make people happy. "The circus people we saw were mature deviants: the frog boy and the two-faced cow and the little girl with the claws for hands. Only, it doesn't make sense. Those people were real and they existed years before the Devastation. Why were they like that?"

Tamara runs her fingers lightly through Shay's hair, combing back curls. "I think we've forgotten. Sometimes, nature gets things mixed up all on its own. Even without toxins left behind by chemical bombs or human beings casually discarding garbage into rivers and streams, our genes and chromosomes are imperfect instruments. Mistakes happen."

I kick at loose pebbles in the street. "I guess."

She reaches over and gives my hand a squeeze, causing me to look up. "You didn't like that movie, did you?"

"No."

"Me neither. If I see the girl who gave me those tickets, I'm asking for my earrings back!"

She makes me smile and with a quick hug, she's off to put Shay to bed.

Feeling restless, J.D. and I wander through the streets of Bio-4. I know my way around the biosphere now. Its wide spaces and intersections are familiar to me. But nothing is as familiar as walking side by side with J.D. Without effort, our strides synchronize to each other's pace in a rhythm that's as natural as breathing.

Usually, we walk in silence, but I want to shake off

the sense of unease caused by the movie. Perhaps conversation will help.

"Has Tamara told you about Shay's daddy?"

"No." He darts a glance in my direction. "What's the story?"

"His name was Eric. He and Tamara were living underground at AgTech. Eric was doing research on soil and how it's connected to global climate change. He got sick and died. Tamara thought his sickness might have come from contaminants in the soil he was testing, but Eric swore he was careful. He always wore protective gear; always kept the samples secure. Tamara said men showed up one day asking about Eric's data. She told them he'd kept all his research at the lab."

"Was that the truth?"

"No."

"What happened?"

"Tamara started to feel scared. She thought she was being watched. Then she found out she was pregnant. So she put Eric's research notes in a safe place and joined a group of travelers. When the travelers stopped in Bio-4 to restock supplies, she stayed here to have the baby."

"Does she know what was in his research?"

"She didn't say. But whatever it was, it may have made him sick. And it might be why Shay...is the way she is."

J.D. is quiet, processing this information. Initially, I hadn't given much thought to the fact that Tamara and Shay were alone. They were like so many others.

61

An intact family with a healthy mother and father and healthy children, too—now that would have been unusual. But I can't help being curious about this soil business. If there's something in the soil that killed Eric or caused Shay's mutation, then who's to say that it's even safe to eat the beans growing here in Bio-4?

Eventually, my eyelids grow heavy, and I signal to J.D. that I'm ready to head back toward the camping lot. We take the next turn side by side.

"What does J.D. stand for?" I ask him.

He tips his head back to stare up at the dome, then turns and gives me a wink. "Juvenile Delinquent."

I watch him warily. "Go on."

"Didn't Tuck tell you? We were rowdies together. Whenever I got caught, some official would pull up my file from the databank. There was a flashing icon at the top of the file. It said 'JD'—for Juvenile Delinquent."

This is more believable than his earlier garbage about "Just Deserts" and no doubt has an element of truth in it. Still, there's something in his tone. It sounds too glib, too pat, like he's said it a few too many times. It's a game to him.

I shake my head. "Nope. I don't believe you."

He gives a half-smile and then with a wave he's off to meet Tuck for some nefarious purpose. I enter the lot and notice that Tamara has fallen asleep, her body encircling Shay on the cushion they call a bed. I lean back on my own bedroll, my eyes soft on the dome above me. At night, it feels like I'm in a moonlit bowl. This barrier between me and the sky is filtered, providing only a dim, diffused light during the day and the merest hint of starlight at night. The moon is still there though, a bright distortion in the dark.

Lately, I've found myself thinking about my mother. I remember so little. Watching Tamara sing Shay softly to sleep each night awakens shadowy impressions from my past, hugs and lullabies I thought I'd lost. After so long without anything, I suddenly recall caresses and comfort. The memories bring both heartache and joy.

I have memories now of my mother's hair, swinging down in a dark veil whenever she reached down to pick me up. And sometimes I think I remember her laughter, open and full of warmth. But I remember sadness, too, and I don't know why. That's when I turn my thoughts away, to Slag.

What will I find there? Desolation, certainly. But will there be memories of my mother there, imprinted somewhere on the landscape? And will I recognize them when I see them? Are there places I've been? Horizons I've seen? Will images from my dreams suddenly fit themselves like lost puzzle pieces onto a scene before me?

Of course, there's also the task I've set for myself. The lake. The sheer idea of it is daunting, to refill the basin that once provided one-fifth of the world's fresh water. It will be a far cry from the tiny puddles and sinkholes I've created so far. But if I can do this one thing, it will be enough.

10

On my day off, I hang out in our space, stretched on my bedroll reading a borrowed book. It's quiet. Tamara and the baby are at the market. J.D. is at the farm. Most of the other campers are out at jobs. I like my days off, the monotony of them, when I can enjoy peace and quiet. Today, my peace and quiet is fleeting.

I look up at the sound of pounding feet and J.D. nearly falls over me in his haste, his breath coming in great, gulping pants.

"We've got to get out of here. Now!" He grabs up his bedroll, a pair of socks, and his backpack.

"What's the matter?" I haven't moved from my spot on the bedroll. I watch in amazement as J.D. hurriedly gathers up his belongings. "Slow down."

"There's a man with a mustache," he says quickly, biting down on each word. "He's showing your picture in town."

I try to digest this, absently aware of the fact that I've never seen J.D. rattled before. Even when he first saw me making water, he was excited, but accepting. This is different. He resumes his packing while I try to make sense of what he's just said. It must be a mistake. Who on earth would have a picture of me, let alone be trying to find me?

"You must have imagined it," I say, finally. "There is absolutely no man who would be looking for me."

"I'm not imagining it. He had your picture. I saw it."

"Oh." I frown, searching my memory, trying to figure who it could be. I'm clueless. "Who do you think he is?"

'He looked official. He had the suit of a territory official and a photo of you. I'd gone into town to make a few purchases, to pick up pans for the farm. There I was, standing in line with these pans in my hand, and this man is in front of me, showing *your* photo to the shop owner."

"There must be some mistake. I can't think of anyone...unless...."

J.D. stops what he's doing and looks at me with narrowed eyes. "Unless what?"

I shrug, trying to laugh it off. "I don't know why it never occurred to me. Of course, I've never known anyone who left before."

"What are you talking about?"

"The orphanage must have reported me missing," I say, keeping my voice calm. J.D. knew I'd run away from the Garner Home for Girls, but not much more than that. "Of course, I can't imagine why Matron would go to the trouble. It's not like she harbored fond feelings for me. But how else could this man have a photo of me?"

I try not to show it, but I'm shaken by the knowledge that someone's looking for me. It's unexpected and inconvenient. I like being at Bio-4. It's been a nice breather, a source of food and shelter and human interaction. But—I give J.D. a long look then start packing up my backpack—it's no longer safe.

"We can't leave without saying good-bye to Tamara," I tell him.

"We don't have time."

"She'll worry about us if she comes back and we've just disappeared. I have to say good-bye, J.D. I have to kiss Shay...." My voice breaks. The enormity of what we're doing hits me. We're going to leave this place for good. And I'm going to leave people I love. This is a new experience for me.

"Fine," he agrees, reluctantly, "but you have to hurry. We don't know how much of Bio-4 this guy's covered or if there are more people out there like him, showing your picture to shopkeepers. Someone may recognize you."

We finish packing and head toward the street market. Both of us keep our eyes peeled, anxiously scanning passersby for any sign of J.D.'s man with the mustache. For the first time since our arrival here, everyone looks suspicious, and I shrink into myself, trying to be invisible. Every time I see a man who looks official, I tense, my stomach clenching.

Finally, we spot Tamara. She's kneeling on a large blanket with Baby Shay on her lap. Beside her, a small rack holds bracelets, necklaces and earrings fashioned out of polished stones. I have one of her pieces, an anklet, which Tamara made for me out of golden Tiger Eye beads. I treasure it.

"What's wrong?" she says at once, perceiving our alarm.

"We're leaving."

"Now?"

"Right now." I reach out and hug her, then bend down to plant a kiss on the soft cheek of Baby Shay. Her dark, solemn eyes gaze unblinkingly at me with trust and innocence. My heart shudders, breaks. Will I ever see her again?

"If anyone comes around asking about me, just say...." At a loss, I glance at J.D.

"...just say you spent time with us briefly when we were in town," he finishes for me, "but we never confided in you where we were going or what our plans were."

"It's true," she says softly. "You never have."

"Bye, Tamara," I whisper, giving her another swift tug. She hugs me hard, and I can't hold back the tears sneaking out the corner of my eyes to slide down my cheeks.

"Be safe."

I nod, jerkily.

"We've got to go, Kira," says J.D.

I know he's right and with one last, wet smile for the baby, I follow him out of the market. My eyes are so filled with tears I can barely see where we're going. This is hard, so much harder than taking that first step away from the orphanage.

Turning a corner, I spot the fortune-teller's shop, the one I visited my first day in Bio-4. I wipe my eyes and place a hand on J.D.'s arm, slowing him down. "Remember I told you about the strange fortune teller woman? That's her place, there." The old woman is standing in the doorway of her shop, her white eyes staring in our direction. I turn to J.D. "I've already had my palm read," I tell him, trying to temper my anxiety with humor, "maybe you should give it a try, get a psychic reading for luck before we hit the road."

He turns to glance where I'm pointing. At that moment I realize the woman with the white eyes is not looking at us, she is looking beyond us. Hairs prickling on the back of my neck, I turn, locking eyes with a man standing across the marketplace. The look of startled recognition in his dark gaze is sufficient for me to know who he is, even before I register the mustache and the attire of a territory official.

I must have transmitted my alarm to J.D. because he snaps his head around in time to see the man pointing in my direction and shouting to someone. Not taking the time to see whom he's shouting to or if there are more than just the two of them, J.D. and I shrink back into the crowd, darting between bodies.

"He doesn't know you, J.D.," I shout, in between panting breaths as we dodge and weave out of sight. "We've got to split up."

"No!"

"Yes! Listen to me. Maybe I can create a diversion to focus attention elsewhere. Then it will be easier to exit the dome unnoticed." Snaking as fast as we can through the crowd, we slip down a side alley. Ahead is the hemp

68

factory. My idea is immediate and awful. Perhaps the idea is immediate because the scenario I'm envisioning has played out so many times in my bored, factory girl daydreams that it feels inevitable. "J.D., I know what I'm going to do. We have to split right now. You go to the farm. Act like everything is normal. I'll meet you there."

He glances at me uncertainly. Sweat is pouring down his face and his shirt is soaked with it. "Are you sure you know what you're doing?"

"No. Just go."

He gives me a final look then pivots in the other direction, pounding down the pavement toward the perimeter.

Taking a deep breath, I slip around the corner of the factory and enter through the employee entrance. Trying to compose myself, I swipe my arm across my face and settle my breath.

Starting a fire is one of the worst crimes. Every thing, every place is so dry and fires can quickly spin out of control. If I get caught, there'll be hell to pay. All the fire-fighting chemicals require a mixture of seawater and dry chemical powder for activation. Seawater is not purely drinkable, but it is no less precious in these times and must be brought in through miles of pipeline to the Biosphere.

Taking the stairs toward the second floor, I hear someone approaching, and I try to compose my features into an expression of nonchalance.

"I didn't know you were working today," says a familiar voice, a woman from the soap-making room.

"I had something I needed to do," I reply vaguely.

On the second floor, I check to make sure no one's around, before slipping into a storage area. The air is thick with dust and lint and floating particles of hemp.

I pull a matchbox from my backpack. Striking a match against the side of the box, I drop it onto a stack of baled fibers, slated for weaving. Braided cord is stacked alongside giant spools of yarn and crates of unpolished twine. The material ignites, becoming a slow smolder then gradually spreading. I fan the flames, coughing as I raise a halo of smoke.

Carefully, I stick my head out the door. Before I raise an alarm, I want to make sure there's enough of a fire to draw a crowd of bystanders. Maybe if people's attention is focused on putting out a fire, the search for a single runaway won't matter.

Seeing no one in the hall, I enter one of the knitting areas, the floor lined wall to wall with heavy looms. I sidle over to a corner crowded with racks of garments. Hidden behind a wall of hemp shirts and trousers, I start another flame, making sure there's plenty of fuel to feed the fire as it spreads. Slipping out of the corner, I move to the wall and yank the alarm.

A searing wail fills the building and shouts of "smoke!" and "fire!" advance around the room. Fear and confusion spreads among the workers and they gaze around uncertainly before rushing toward the nearest exits. I join a group of loom operators, all heading for a back stairwell. I let myself be swept along, my eyes watering from the increasing thickness of the smoke.

The press of people against my body has me chok-ing for air and room. I fight back a clutching panic. If I stumble, I'll be trampled. What if I don't make it out in time? What if others don't? I take a breath and hold it and, finally, the press of people carries me out the door to the sidewalk. Hacking now, grabbing at a stitch in my side, I stumble forward, my head kept low.

The sidewalks are mobbed, everyone shouting ad-vice and warnings to the approaching fire fighters. The dome keeps the smoke from dissipating and until the fire fighters can get the dome's ventilation system ad-justed, there's precious little visibility. Soon everyone is hidden in a thick cloud of ash. One man raises his arm to point toward a second floor window where smoke is pouring out in black billows, and I dart beneath him toward the back of the crowd and freedom.

When I get to the farm, J.D. is pacing behind one of the outbuildings. He turns toward me, then stops, his expression one of amazement at the sight of me striding up the gravel. I glance down at myself and realize I'm filthy from head to toe, completely unrecognizable.

"I got caught in a fire."

Reaching out a finger, he swipes it down my cheek. When he lifts his hand, his finger is covered in black soot. "No kidding." He casts a quick glance down the path. "Were you followed?"

"Of course not." I grab his hand, not caring that I'm getting him dirty. I need the physical connection. "Don't you want to know what I did? Whether anyone's hurt?"

"Are they?"

71

I frown. "I don't know. I tried to set the alarm early enough for everyone to get out. But what if someone didn't...."

"I'm sure you were careful. You probably triggered the alarm even earlier than you had to—everyone's safe."

It occurs to me that he doesn't want me to feel badly, and I'm struck by a surge of gratitude. I hope he's right and everyone really did make it out in time.

He wipes sooty fingers down his britches then hitches his backpack over his shoulders. "Are you ready to go?"

I nod and we head off-road toward the area farms. We stick to the vegetated areas as long as we can, but soon we're back among the rivers of sand and dust, narrow cracks giving way to ragged sections of dry, hard sod. Our pace slows as we settle in for the next stage of our journey.

11

"How long were you at the orphanage?" J.D. asks.

"Almost as long as I can remember." My mind slips backward, reaching as far as I know how to take it, to before I even had language skills to organize my thoughts, when memories were just motion or color; sound or smell. "I have so few memories of my mother. Although..."

"What?"

I clear my throat. I need this. I need the distraction of conversation. Tonight, the moon is a slit in the sky, illuminating a silvery sheathe of sand. J.D. is a shadow beside me, the outline of something solid through which starlight cannot pass. I know his eyes are searching the landscape, his body taut and electric, wired for whatever action may be required. We're both tense since leaving Bio-4.

"Sometimes I dream about her," I say softly. "I wake up, and I've got this feeling, like her voice or her smell or her touch was somehow close to me, and by waking up, I've caused that to disappear. It makes me sad."

"So you weren't a baby when you went to the

orphanage?"

"No."

This doesn't make me particularly unusual. Many children do arrive at the orphanages as infants. People are so terribly short-lived. There's often no accounting for who lives and who doesn't. The strange interactions between human genes and toxins left lingering in the air and soil and water create abnormalities in the body and each new generation is just a little more fragile than the one before it. Even if a child doesn't start his or her life at a children's home, it's where most children eventually end up.

There was another orphanage not far from the Garner Home that took in mutant babies. Cook was from there. She always remembered it as a sad place. Most of the babies didn't survive. Cook wasn't born with a big mutation, just a small one, a sort of tail. Doctors were able to remove it.

I can tell J.D.'s waiting for more information, but there's really nothing unusual in my history. "Until the age of five, I lived with an uncle." I haven't thought of him in ages. "I don't remember him well." I continue slowly, "but I know he was a large man with red hair, and he used to twirl me in his arms to make me laugh. We lived by the ocean, and I can remember walking with him on the beach. He never let me touch anything. He was afraid of contamination, so he made me wear these oversized boots and gloves."

I'm unable to hold back a chuckle, recalling how it took me four steps for every one stride of his. He'd swing me onto his shoulders when I got too tired to keep up.

"What happened to him?"

"He harvested kelp for a living. He and his crew would go out for days at a time on this harvesting barge. He only took me onboard once because I was so frightened by the giant blades they used to cut the kelp. One day, he and his crew went out to sea and never came back." I keep the sigh out of my voice and tighten my hold on the strap of my pack. I don't want it to seem like I'm asking for sympathy. Many people are alone in the world. J.D.'s alone. But he and I kind of have each other now, don't we? "I was staying with a neighbor when my uncle disappeared. One day, a man came and got me and took me to the orphanage."

"Do you remember the man?"

I concentrate for a moment, but fail to come up with a clear picture. "I must have been overwhelmed or confused. I don't know. I don't have a clear image. I do remember arriving at the Garner Home and meeting Matron and being put into a room filled with other girls my age. I was terrified."

"And there's no other family? There's no great-aunt somewhere who might be trying to find you?"

"No," I tell him, ignoring my sense of isolation. "There's no one."

We walk awhile longer in silence then I figure it's my turn. "J.D.?"

"Hmm?"

"What are you looking for?"

He gives me a puzzled glance. "What do you mean?"

"I'm just trying to figure out what you're doing." I don't add "with me," although I wonder that, too. "You've traveled all sorts of places. What are you looking for?"

For the longest time, I think he's not going to answer. He forges ahead, his eyes intent on where he's going. "I'm not looking for anything, Kira. I don't see the point in it. I'm surviving one day at a time, the same as the next guy."

"Oh." I'm disappointed. What had I expected? Poetry? Some sort of declaration. Sheesh. Well, survival is what we're all doing, one way or the other. But if it's survival that matters to him, why not stay in the Biosphere?

"Wouldn't it be easier if you just…."

"No. It wouldn't," he says, apparently adding mind reader to his array of talents.

A few miles later, he clears his throat. "I want to try and answer your question again."

"Okay."

More minutes pass. I wait.

"You asked me what I'm looking for, and I am looking to survive, that's true enough," he says slowly. "But, deep down, I know there's more to it. I think I'm also looking for a *reason* to survive."

"I'm not sure I understand. Survival's an instinct. Every living thing has an instinct to survive."

"Let me put it another way. Everybody dies. Nobody gets off the hook on that one, right? And it's my belief that we all die the same death. No matter how you live your life, no matter what you believe, death is death. So

76

if we're all going to die regardless, what does it matter if we die off slowly, one by one in a trickle, or whether we die off in one generation of mass extinction?"

"Oh. I see."

"If I'm going to die; if you're going to die...."

I'm unable to suppress my wince.

"It's not clear to me why I should be invested in the human race, in human survival—or even in my own survival. Does any of it matter?"

I don't know the answer to his question. Maybe death *is* the same for everybody. But life is not. Maybe it's only our life and what we do with it that makes us unique. Regardless of how I twist it around in my mind, it seems like life should matter. That he matters and I matter. That life is a gift even now in this time of desolation and affliction. I just don't know why.

"Since I met you," he continues softly, "it feels a little easier to wake up each morning and keep walking. So I'm willing to consider that there's something I haven't figured out yet and traveling with you may help me to find it."

He gives me a small smile, which I try to return. His words aren't exactly a declaration, but they're honest. And oddly enough, I feel better.

It occurs to me that my being followed could put his chances of survival at risk, which is a compelling reason why he and I should split up. But more than ever, I don't want to be alone. And maybe he doesn't want to be alone either. Circumstances and, if I'm being honest, a difficult personality made me a loner at the Garner Home. Now I've discovered I enjoy the company of others. Certain others, anyway. Tamara and Shay had felt like family, at least like what I imagine family to be. I miss them already. And J.D. is, well, I'm not sure what he is, but he's important.

The next few days are tough.

I wonder if J.D. knows the tiny hairs on the back of my neck frequently stand on end, for no apparent reason. Does he feel my watchfulness? I feel his. We move and move, barely stopping to rest. There's a tight ball in my stomach now, forcing me to pick up my pace.

"Whoever that was looking for me, do you think he's given up?"

"It's been ages since you left the orphanage, Kira. If he's been looking for you since you left, clearly he's not the type who gives up easily."

"Do you think he knows how long we were at Bio-4?"

"I've thought about that," J.D. says. "He would have checked the camping lots. There are security cameras at all of them. I don't know how long they hold onto the footage, but we're definitely on those tapes, Kira. He would have seen us."

"And Tamara and the baby."

"Yes."

This shuts me up. I worry about them. I worry about their safety. I could never forgive myself if something bad happened to them because they'd been our friends. Yet, how would I know? And why did I assume

78

the man hunting me would even be interested in them? Then again, I was still trying to figure out why he would be interested in *me*.

"GPS shows a small lake bed ahead," I say, slapping away a fly. "Do you think I could make water? A bath would be nice."

"It's not safe."

"You don't know that."

"If this guy knows you can make water...."

"Why would he? Only Mary knew," I insist, "and no one believed her."

"We have to think the way they're thinking," says J.D.

"'They?' What 'they?'" I vent, throwing up my hands in frustration. "There's no 'they.' There's a guy with a photo, looking for a runaway."

"Maybe."

Suddenly, we stop in our tracks. A strange humming sound seems to be getting louder and I glance around in alarm. In seconds, a swarm of stinging flies has surrounded us.

"Head for the rocks," shouts J.D., pointing toward an outcrop in the distance.

I break into a run, slapping furiously at the pests landing on my neck and cheeks and hands. They even brush against my eyeballs, craving the moisture there. The bugs seem bent on attacking any exposed skin. My eyes are tearing, my mind clouded by the stinging pain. And so it is that I stumble into an ambush, snatched up by rough hands. My fists flail wildly against flesh and bone before a blow to the head sinks me into darkness.

12

I hear mutterings and giggling in the background, but I'm reluctant to open my eyes until I've got a better idea of my situation. How long have I been unconscious? My head feels like it's wrenched in a vice. My throat is raw. My body aches. I try to wiggle my fingers and realize part of my discomfort is due to ropes tied around my wrists and ankles.

It's all I can do not to scream with frustration. I am so brainless. I thought there was danger behind me, perhaps ahead of me, but I hadn't been alert to the danger that was close at hand. Had our attackers released the flies on us? Or had that merely been a happy coincidence for them? And where was J.D.?

"Fresh meat. Fresh meat."

A childish, sing-songy voice sends a shiver through me. Cautiously, I peer beneath my lashes. I'm in a cave, that's obvious. I smell smoke. Firelight casts moving shadows on rock walls. There's a person standing near me. In the firelight, I can make out thin, emaciated legs. Black fingernails on a sallow hand reach toward me.

"Don't touch me!"

The man jerks back his hand, startled. I open my eyes and try to twist myself upright. Glancing around I see half a dozen gaunt faces staring at me. Some young. Some adolescent. All show clear signs of advanced skin cancer. Dark melanomas on the face. Oozing moles. I'm torn between revulsion and reluctant sympathy. Someone has opened my backpack on the cave floor and they've been gorging themselves on the trail mix and algae bars packed inside. *There go my supplies,* I realize numbly.

The man towers over me, frowning. "You are spunky, hmm?" His eyes rake me top to bottom. "At least you look to be in good health," he says shortly.

"Where's J.D.?"

"The boy then? Why he got away. Took a bite out of my ear, he did, the little monster." The man turns, showing me a bloody wound on the side of his head.

Repulsed by the ragged tear in the man's ear, I'm nevertheless flooded with relief. Thank goodness, J.D.'s okay. He got away. Now how can I do the same?

"What do you want with me?"

"Why my family and me, we want you for dinner," he says grinning. The others snicker.

I take their meaning. I'm the fresh meat. I've heard stories of course, of bandits and scavengers and other outcasts who dine on the weak and the dying. A trembling begins deep inside me that I try desperately to mask. I mustn't let them see my fear. And I'm not weak. I'm not defenseless. My body threatens to betray me, but I fight for a measure of control. I have no intention

81

of being anybody's dinner.

I search the room for an idea, for a way out, for something. A pile of bones in a dark corner catches my eye. Are they human bones? My stomach churns and I glance away, my eyes settling on the faces watching me. One or two are openly hostile. The others just look gaunt, pleading, hungry.

"It's wrong," I say stupidly, my eyes searching out the man's. Are you supposed to make eye contact with a predator? I have no idea, but I'm desperate to connect with him on some level.

"What is this 'wrong?' Who says it is wrong? We do what is necessary to survive. Survival is a good thing. Survival is right."

What about my survival?

"You could go to the Biosphere," I say, scrambling for something to change their minds. "There are people there who could help you. They could take care of your sores. Maybe you could get a job. There'd be food."

"Beh! Who you kidding? There's nothin' in the Biosphere for us. Once you get sick, the Territory puts you on the docket for euthanasia. As far as they're concerned, we're the walking dead. We can't get a water ration. We can't get jobs. They get one look at us, and we'll be rounded up like animals."

I'm not unmoved. Life is hard for everybody, but for these people every day is misery. Still, my life is at stake. It takes me a minute to realize I have only one bargaining chip. My palms are damp with fear, but my mouth is dry. Now that's odd, I note absently, for someone who makes water. I force my mind to the task at hand. "What if I could give you water, enough water for your entire family?"

"What foolishness is this? Girlie, there's not enough water in your pack to last one day."

"No. Listen. I can *make* water. Truly. I can give you water out of the ground. I can fill a small pond or a pool here in the cave. I'll show you."

He looks at me suspiciously. The others have grown quiet. "What are you saying, hmm?"

"You don't even have to untie my hands. Just take the ropes off my ankles. And you can come with me. I just need...." I search for a depression in the cave floor. "Is there a ditch or an old sinkhole nearby? It may take a few minutes, but I promise I can do it. If you can just be patient. Is there something, a place I can make water?"

"You're playing games with me. If I untie you, you will try to escape. You will attack my last good ear then make a run for it." He claps his hands together, causing me to jump. "I knew I should have thumped you harder. Your throat could be slit by now. Thaddeus, bring me my knife."

"No games," I insist, struggling to hold onto my composure. I won't be the victim they want me to be. "I can help you. Just tell me if there's a dried up spring around here."

"Weell, there used to be a pool in the next chamber, seepage from above, you know, in the ancient days. It is nothing now, of course...dry, dry."

"Show me."

For a long moment he's silent, rubbing his jaw. "I have seen strange things," he says finally. "I have seen people who glow in the dark. I have seen babies born with fins and flippers in a place that has no water. Perhaps you speak the truth."

He motions to a tall, thin boy with hard eyes. "Thad, untie her."

The boy inches forward to cut the ropes at my feet. A dark sore covers his cheek, but it's the blatant hunger in his eyes that has me turning my head away. I stretch my legs slowly, wincing with pain as the blood returns to my extremities. Slowly, I stand, pressing my bound hands against the rock wall for support. I feel lightheaded, and it's a moment before I can walk.

My captor leads the way past the small fire. The others step back to let me pass. At the back of the cavern there's a small opening in the wall, near the ground.

"That is it," he says. "In there. You can tell if you poke your head in a bit."

I lie down on my belly and poke my head through the hole. Sure enough, there's what looks like an old pool basin, surrounded by crumbling stalagmites. The back wall actually looks like a waterfall that has been turned to stone. From one end to the other, the depression looks to be about sixty feet long and maybe four feet deep, bigger than anything I've tried to fill.

Here, for a moment, out of sight of their prying eyes I let myself feel fully the dark sweat of fear. Exhaling softly, I bring my fingers to the lip of the basin and wish for water. Behind me, I can hear the others whispering.

The man nudges my leg. "What are you doing in there? Do not be playing games."

"No games. Just hold on," I mutter.

In a minute, I see what I'm waiting for, a small dark stain starting to grow against the ground and I am exhilarated. It hits me that this may be the first time I have truly taken delight in my ability.

I slither out backwards and motion for the man to take my place. He gestures to the boy, Thad, to keep an eye on me. I feel safer with the wall at my back and face him and the room, all of us watching each other warily. Even though I'm relieved that J.D. escaped capture, a part of me wishes he were here by my side.

In a minute the man slides out and stands, raking his hands through thinning hair. He casts a look at me, pursing his lips thoughtfully. "This is a good thing you can do."

Thad drops down and pokes his head into the opening to see for himself. When he stands, his eyes look uncertain, but his voice is hard. "Now we eat her."

"No," says my captor shortly, but his eyes on me are thoughtful. "Now we trade her. Tomorrow. We will do it tomorrow."

I'm stunned. "What? But I thought...."

"That I would let you go?" he answers. "No. You have saved your life. My family will not eat you. But we will get value in exchange for you—food and medicine. These things we need very much. Now, we eat."

My hands are kept tied, but my feet are allowed to stay unbound. With all eyes on me, I can't make a move without it being registered. I sit against the cave wall and the smallest of them brings over a small bowl. Small boys should be round and chubby, but this child has protruding ribs and thin matchstick legs that barely support him.

"Food. Food," he whispers, reaching into the bowl and holding out a dead beetle and what looks like a piece of root. "Eat. Mmm, good. No pasty sides."

Baffled, I look at one of the girls.

"No pesticides," she translates.

"How does he know?"

She shrugs one thin shoulder. "Maybe he doesn't."

I take the bug and crunch down hungrily. The child smiles with approval. He puts the bowl down where I can reach it with my bound hands. Then, he does something unexpected. He leans over and kisses me gently on the forehead. I'm startled. Have I ever been kissed? I have no memory of it. Nevertheless, I feel a surge of tenderness. I smile at him and he smiles back.

"You smell good," he says. Then he reaches his hand into the waistband of his pants and pulls out a photo. My mother's picture. He places the photo in my lap and goes back to the fire. The others watch closely, but no one interferes.

My wrists are still tied, but I pick up the photo and look at it before putting it awkwardly in my shirt pocket. It was the one thing in my backpack that served no functional purpose, but it was also the one thing I'd be most sad to lose.

Stomach growling, I eat. There are only a few beetles in the bowl. Hardly enough to take the edge off my hunger. I am made aware of how thin is the thread that keeps this small family group alive. After I've eaten, I'm brought a bowl of water from the pool I've made. The others wait for me to drink, then seeing it's safe, drink themselves.

Once everyone's done eating, I'm ignored. The others take turns peeking at the newly-formed pool of water, then they huddle together talking, about my fate perhaps; about the things they will receive in exchange for me. Will they trade me to the man with the mustache? Or are there people in this wilderness who have things of value to offer for a girl who can make water?

Speaking of making water. "Excuse me," I interrupt.

"What do you want?" the man asks.

"I have to, ah, you know." I can't believe I'm blushing "I have to pee."

I can see his wheels turning. Evidently, he comes to the conclusion that he doesn't need to recycle my urine since he now has an adequate supply of water in the cave. He points at the oldest boy. "Thad, take her outside."

"You can't be serious?"

"And Belinda, you go, too," he adds, addressing the oldest girl. Perhaps she is to keep the closest eye on me as I go about nature's business. How am I going to get away from both of them?

"Sheesh."

My little friend hops up. "Me, too," he says brightly.

Thad grabs a club leaning against the wall and motions to the others to join him. It is a ragtag group that escorts me out of the cave.

13

The little boy slips his frail hand into my bound hand. I close my fingers awkwardly around his. There's something about this child. He's too trusting. How will he fare in this world?

"He's coming," he whispers to me, his face angled up to mine.

I glance at the others, but the two of them are deep in conversation. Thad catches my eyes on him and leers, swinging his weapon threateningly. Quickly, I turn to look at the girl. She's paused, her eyes scanning the landscape.

"Who's coming?" I whisper back. "J.D.? My friend?"

He nods sagely.

"How do you know?"

"Smell it. Smell him."

"Ah." I gaze at him in wonder. I take a good sniff myself, but smell nothing but the flat, metallic taste of the air. "What's your name?"

"Me? Joey."

"My name is Kira, Joey. It's nice to meet you."

"Kira," he says. He catches my eye. "I'll remember."

I'm led to a patch of scrub barely thick enough to shield me from the waist down. Thad gives me a shove. "Go here."

I edge behind the small covering, trying to be discreet. I sneak a peek at my surroundings as best I can, but see no sign of J.D. Shoot. Where is he? I can't see him, I certainly can't smell him, but I find myself believing the boy, Joey. J.D. is out here somewhere. He hasn't left me behind. With my wrists bound, I'd never be able to get away from my guards on my own.

Suddenly, I hear a whirring sound. My head jerks around in time to see a large rock whiz past me and strike Thad in the back of the head. He groans and claps his hands to his skull. I take advantage of the sudden distraction to dart out of the scrub and dash across the hard ground in the opposite direction, ignoring the shouts behind me. I hear more stones hurling past me. Great day in the morning, does J.D. have an entire arsenal at his disposal?

"Bye, Kira!" calls little Joey, breathlessly, behind me. "Bye, bye!"

"Bye, Joey," I call back. I can hear his brother and sister swearing behind me, fumbling to get out of the way of the sudden onslaught, followed by the occasional gasp when a rock finds its mark.

Quickly, I'm swallowed up by the darkness, and I slow my steps, becoming hesitant.

"J.D., where are you?"

"Here."

He jumps down from a boulder, the cheeky grin on

his face barely discernible by starlight. A slingshot hangs loosely from one hand. With the other, he pulls a stone from his pocket and places it in the sling. "Should I keep going?"

I press my bound hands against his arm. "I don't want you to hit the little boy."

"Nah. Mostly I've been aiming at the ugly brute with the bat."

"How can you even see them from here?"

He clambers back up the boulder and searches the darkness. "They're running back the way you came."

"Good. Let's go quickly before they get the others. I want to get away from here."

He jumps back down, his eyes searching my face. "Are you okay?"

I laugh weakly. "I'm fine. They've got my backpack, though. The GPS, my bedroll, all the food and sunscreen...."

"Forget it."

I glance around, my eyes hunting for something that looks familiar. Was the path we were on earlier over to my left? "I don't know where we are."

"I know. Follow me."

J.D. cuts the ropes binding my hands and we set off at a brisk trot. Soon he has us back on course, heading north. Once we've covered a little distance and confirmed that we're not being followed, I'm overcome with nausea and stop to throw up my guts, the thin remains of my bug dinner. With shaky breath, I quickly relate what happened between the ambush and J.D.'s rescue. I don't tell him how scared I was. When I finish recounting my tale, he reaches over and gives my hair a tug. I feel better.

Every moment from then on becomes one of wary watchfulness. Every minute. Every hour. I feel it deep in my bones now, the danger; the following. Is it the man from the Biosphere? Hungry bandits who want to exploit my ability to insure their own survival? Or is it my imagination? I don't say a word to J.D. Maybe he knows. Maybe he feels it too.

"Thank you," I say to him finally.

He looks at me, baffled. "For what?"

"For rescuing me. For not just leaving me, you know, back there."

"What? And let them make stew out of you? They have no idea how lucky they are. I'm sure you would have given them terrible indigestion. Hmm..." he says slowly. "On second thought, maybe I should have left you there."

"Since when do you have a sense of humor?" I throw a punch at his shoulder and he dodges it, muffling a snort of laughter.

We travel at night and sleep during the day, taking turns sharing the one bedroll while the other finds a sheltered place to stand guard. When I do sleep, it's fitful. My exhausted body falls heavily into slumber even though I dread the moment when my subconscious takes over my mind. Day after day, I sink into ethereal, bone white dreams that leave me cold and shaking, even when it's a hundred degrees outside. Why this anxiety?

I still feel followed, watched. Maybe the bandits were a warning that my time is running out.

Early one evening, J.D. and I stumble across a small air system, the wind kicking up dancing dirt devils. Thin flumes twist and turn in the air and we shield our eyes as we cross through, coughing from the dust, yet captivated by the atmospheric show before us.

We're approaching the Dead Lakes Region now and we tramp through dry washes that have not run with water in years—only the faded memory of water remains. I am becoming more adept at recognizing the places that have known water. There's something in the pitch of the land, in the striations of color and flow across the bedrock. I try to grasp the realization that I've almost reached my goal. It's no longer some distant, uncertain thing. It's near and immediate.

Before our stopover at Bio-4, I'd been making water with impunity, filling small ponds and roadside ditches, calling forth liquid from some primeval tear in the universe. Not anymore. J.D. has convinced me that every filled well and water puddle is like an arrow pointing directly at us, making our path transparent to anyone in pursuit. I don't know if he's right or not. But I feel the following.

Our supplies are low so we're on a ration system, swallowing our measly portion of water every day. In addition, J.D. and I recycle our urine, recapturing the vitamins and minerals we can't afford to let spill on the ground. The trick is to drink immediately while it's still sterile, before there's any contamination. It's warm and salty and, as much as I detest the taste, it's never enough. I go to bed thirsty. I wake up thirsty. Always thirsty, dry skin clings to my bones like thin parchment.

How can someone capable of calling forth water be so completely dry?

14

We're here. Slag. Tall buildings rise before us in the distance, looking like the interconnected skeleton of something that was once alive. It's strange looking, eerie, but there's a sense of familiarity, too. It feels like a place I once knew—a shadowy landscape in my memory—or maybe not my memory, maybe my mother's, passed to me in some intangible way. Or it could just be the faint recollection of a photo I saw once in a school lesson. J.D. pauses beside me, taking in the scene. It's desolate. Nothing moves.

"Do you want to go now," he asks, "or wait?"

"Do you have the masks?"

He nods.

"We might as well go on," I decide.

Among the supplies J.D. acquired for us at Bio-4 are two respirators. He hands me one now, and I fit it carefully over my face before we approach the city. I don't know how much protection these things provide, but if they keep out even a portion of the invisible toxins in the air, they've served a purpose. It's awkward breathing through the mask. I fight a feeling of claustrophobia, an

94

urge to gasp in a huge lungful of air, and instead make myself breathe normally.

We cross a bridge that's concrete and beautifully carved and arched across what was once a wide river-bed. The bed is dry, just the outline remains, but I can imagine the way it once looked, when people crossed the bridge every day and enjoyed a view of the water.

We walk down quiet streets, past bombed skyscrapers and apartment buildings with windows blasted out. The street is littered with broken glass and debris and we have to constantly pause and check before we place our feet down in front of us. There's a wind here, too, a lonely, desolate movement of air whistling between the buildings.

A teacher once told me that the Devastation was a complete breakdown of civilization, pitting every kind of individual against his or her opposite. Believers against unbelievers. The "haves" versus the "have-nots". Intellectuals against laborers. Even men and women took arms against each other at one point in the fray. It was that idea of "other" that created constantly shift-ing loyalties among groups and unleashed every kind of weapon in the world.

But long before simmering tensions had erupted, the places where J.D. and I had trod had been a heart-land: the breadbasket of the world, ripe with wheat and corn and grassy meadows. That period of history was now the stuff of legends—a time of self-absorption, in-tolerance and greed. But there are consequences. If his-tory teaches us nothing else, it teaches us that. There are always consequences.

We follow the shape of the riverbed and when it curves around to the west, we curve with it, then stop in our tracks at the sight before us. We're standing on Lake Shore Drive and stretching as far as the eye can see is a huge—that's not the word for it, *gargantuan*—dry basin. There's a gradual depression across the road, where the shell of a once-thriving marina still stands. Just past the marina, the scene changes. The land drops steeply into a dark abyss stretching far to the north.

The moon is setting, and I slip off my mask to take a quick breath. It's not as bad as I thought it would be. I catch the faintest trace of airborne chemical underpinning the smell of hot sand. Chlorine. It's present in the air, the soil; easily converting to dioxins and taking up insidious abode in human tissue.

I look past the city perimeter to surrounding foothills, bare and alien. An alkali dust storm is gathering above the old lakebed. There'll be heavy particulates in the air tomorrow. We need to find a safe place indoors.

Drawn by the surreal scene before me, I turn my eyes back to the lake. I find it odd that it's still referred to as 'the lake,' identified by its absent properties. This territory has gone from city to sagebrush and the people have all dispersed. It is not a healthy place.

Following my lead, J.D. pulls off his own mask then nudges me. "Are you going to make water, now?"

"I guess."

"Maybe it would clean the air too. Get rid of some of the dust stirring."

"Yeah."

I don't move. I stand staring at the basin that once was the hub of a lake system supplying twenty percent of the world's fresh surface water. It's astonishing to see it, to finally be here.

Since the Lakes Region was a closed system, the pollutants that reached the water remained indefinitely. PCBs and DDT, metals like chlordane, mirex, toxaphene—once they hit the water, they had nowhere else to go. But at least, there *was* water. It was toxic, sure, but it could have been cleaned. Then in the wake of the Devastation and escalating environmental crisis, the resulting lack of cloud cover exposed everything and everybody to increased radiation, higher temperatures and dehydration. And then there was a small tectonic shift in the south, not much, but just enough to alter the planet's axis and accelerate global climate change.

I can't take my eyes off the vastness of the scene before me. I'm afraid to make my wish. I know it's ridiculous, because I've done this more times than I can count. The thing is, I've only ever filled small ponds. I hadn't considered the overwhelming enormity of a basin like this. I close my eyes and concentrate. I fill my mind with images of water, not the images of my own experience, of course. I draw on memories of digital images, lakes and cascades viewed through a computer screen. Matron had a hologram of a waterfall that looked as though it would dampen your skin if you stood too close. I picture it now. Time passes. Still, I wait. "I wish for water," I whisper.

97

After awhile, J.D. touches my arm. "Nothing's happening," he says.

I open my eyes and stare below me. He's right. Brown cracked earth stretches as far as the eye can see, but no water, not even the dark stain of water.

"Maybe you're doing something differently."

"I'm doing what I've always done," I grumble. "I wish for the water, and then it's just there."

Of course, I know it's not his fault there's no water. I nibble my lip, trying to determine next steps. Have I come all this way for nothing?

I kneel on the ground and stare intently at the lakebed. "I wish for water."

Nothing happens. Unbidden, the image of the small pink flower back at the Garner Home pops into my mind. Making water was accidental then, and effortless. The water appeared immediately and knew where to go. I miss my flower.

"I wish for the whole lakebed to fill up with water." I wait. "Now." I resist the urge to stamp, to shout, to curse the ground for not responding.

Have I run out? What if I'm only able to produce ten thousand gallons or a hundred thousand gallons of water, and I've already wasted it all on an assortment of piddly little puddles?

"It's a big basin," J.D. says. His voice is matter-of-fact, and I'm grateful. If he offered me pity, I couldn't bear it. "Maybe it won't happen right away, not like the others did. Besides, it's almost morning. We need to find a place to sleep."

He's right. And I'm eager to get away from the sight of the empty lake. Its dry darkness taunts me, ridicules my feeble efforts and my grandiose dreams. Who am I to think I could do something profound? I'm nobody. "This is going to take longer to fill." I say, rising. "That's all. We'll come back this evening."

It takes awhile, but we finally find a place to stay for the night. What was once a lakeside condominium is now a ruin, but less so than some of the other buildings. We climb stairs to an abandoned apartment overlooking the lake. Whatever windows are still intact, we open for ventilation, relying on thick draperies to filter out the worst dust and debris in the air, as well as the harsh sun.

There's furniture, sagging sofas with ripped upholstery and chairs filled with dust; splintered picture frames that look blood-spattered. There's even a bed. But we're used to sleeping on the ground now. We stretch out on the floor, thinly cushioned by a dry, tattered rug. I'm exhausted.

"Kira?"

"Hmm?"

"Earlier, by the lake, you seemed…afraid."

His comment catches me off guard. Hasn't he seen me afraid? I'm afraid all the time. How can he not know that? In the last few months, I've been afraid of the dark, afraid of loneliness, afraid of going hungry, afraid of being found and sent back to the orphanage, even afraid of being eaten. Now, there's a new fear.

"I'm afraid of losing this ability, J.D. It's all I have." There's more, of course, that I don't say, because it's too embarrassing. I don't tell him I wanted to matter, really matter…to someone, to the world, maybe to history. It's foolishness.

Awkwardly, he clears his throat.

"I don't think it's all you have, Kira. Whether or not you can make water, you're still, I mean, you're better than…." He coughs. "Well, you shouldn't be so hard on yourself."

For just a moment, it doesn't matter that I couldn't make the lake fill. Right here, right now, I feel a little less alone.

"What about you?" I whisper, thinking that J.D. probably isn't afraid of anything. He responds without hesitation.

"You scare me," he says bluntly.

"You mean because I'm a mutant." I try to inject a note of humor, but it falls flat.

"Don't be ridiculous. Maybe you are a mutant."

"Hey…"

"But so what? These days, isn't everybody twisted in some way or another? This is different. It's just…." He stumbles for words, raking a hand through his hair. "I'm just saying it's different walking with someone. Walking alone is fine. Walking with you is, well, it changes things is all. Like when you were captured and I didn't know if…." He stops. "Are you tired?" he asks suddenly, changing the subject. "I'm whipped. I'm going to turn in now. G'nite."

He rolls over onto his side and in minutes is breathing evenly. I stare into the dim room, grinning.

100

15

We're awake before nightfall and rise silently. I want to look out the window. I want to open the drapes and see water, miles and miles of it stretching off into the distance, shimmering in the half-light of evening.

I don't. I take a veggie bar out of J.D.'s pack and begin chewing silently.

He just looks at me.

"Are you going to do it, or am I?" he asks, finally.

"You do it."

After a moment, he walks over to the large plate glass window facing the lake. He takes a deep breath then pulls aside the fabric. Without moving from where I sit, I can tell there's nothing. The lack of expression on J.D.'s face gives it away.

He lets the curtain fall back into place and walks over to me, dropping down onto the floor.

"What now?" I ask.

"You try again," he says, reaching into the pack for something to eat.

After we've eaten, we step outside. Deciding not to don our masks right away, we pause to take in our surroundings. The moon is low and bright and clearly reveals the outline of the empty lake basin.

"Let's walk up the lakeshore a ways," I say.

We turn north and begin to hike along the levee. Occasionally, a lizard or cockroach scurries away as we approach, but for the most part, we're alone. It's quiet here, illuminated only by the moon and stars. The buildings of the city loom darkly beside us. After a couple of miles, we arrive at a steel pier stretching out onto the lake.

Reading my mind, J.D. takes my hand and helps me up the broken steps of the pier. Pushing through an old turnstile, we walk slowly toward the far end. Benches line the sides of the pier, and I picture the way it must have been a long time ago, when lovers strolled here or sat to enjoy the view. Maybe there were gulls to feed and old men dropping fishing lines over the side.

The pier is long, but too soon we're at the end. J.D. and I lean forward to look over the railing. It's dark below us, but clearly dry, and a thin wind stirs our hair.

"Go ahead," he whispers. "You can do it."

I gaze at the lake, at the vast emptiness before me, and I whisper the words, the same words I always say. We stand together for a few minutes, but I think neither one of us is surprised this time when nothing happens.

"Maybe we should climb down into the lakebed," he says. "Maybe if you were standing right down in it...."

"I don't know, J.D. I never had to do that before. I can't believe being able to make water was some sort of temporary thing like a cold or a rash."

102

He glances at the twilight sky. "Maybe the stars are out of alignment. The fact that you could make water might have been this giant cosmic accident," he jokes.

I turn, ready to argue, but the words die on my lips. We are found. Standing less than ten feet away, his arms crossed, his lips curved in a faint smile, is the man with the mustache.

"Having trouble, kids?"

I know it's illogical, but my first desire is to bark at this person that we're *not* kids. I might have been when I found my flower at the orphanage, but I'm certainly not now. That much should be obvious.

J.D. turns, slipping cold fingers into mine.

"It didn't work, did it?" the man says, gesturing toward the lake. "Don't feel bad. You're just a little thing, and it's a big lake. Give yourself a few years. It'll come."

"I don't know what you're talking about," I say, forcing my voice to stay calm.

"Of course, you do," he says, softly. "But excuse my bad manners. I haven't introduced myself. My name is Lukas Thorne." He smiles at me. "And you would be Kira." He turns to J.D. "And you would be J.D."

When we step off the pier, we're surrounded by armed men and directed to an armored rover. J.D. and I glance at each other, recognizing the futility of escape. We climb inside, not speaking to the man who climbs in behind us. Unable to see precisely where we're going, it's clearly within the city limits. We only travel a few minutes before reaching our destination.

We're led into an ugly, squat building, about eight stories tall. Photovoltaic panels cover the roof and I spot an algae bio-fuel pump off to the side. We follow the man named Thorne to the third floor and into a small bare room with two beds, a small table and a couple of chairs.

"This will be your room," he says.

We step into the room cautiously and turn to look at him.

"How long are you planning on keeping us here?" I ask.

"There'll be plenty of time for discussion later, Kira. I promise to explain everything. Right now, however, I have an important meeting to attend. Everyone's going to be so pleased that you're safe and sound."

I don't ask the obvious question, which is *Who is everyone?*

"A member of my staff will be stationed outside the door at all times. If you need anything, just let him know. Are you hungry?"

So we're to be guarded. I'm not surprised, although I don't understand the point of it all ... and I *am* hungry. I catch J.D.'s eye, and he gives a barely perceptible nod. "I suppose we could eat," I say.

The barest flicker of a smile crosses our captor's face, and I want to hit him for finding amusement at our expense. Actually, I just want to hit him, period. A good solid punch to the gut.

"I'll have Michael send something up," he says. He turns to leave, then pauses to give me a direct look. "You two may share this room," he says softly. "I know you've been traveling together for a long time, and I can only imagine what you've had to endure. I want you to rest and relax and enjoy three square meals a day. However, if you abuse my hospitality, you'll be separated. Am I clear?"

J.D. and I glance at each other then nod our agreement.

"Good."

As soon as he's gone, we investigate the room. The bed frames are made from solid iron bars. A thin memory foam cushion serves as a mattress. The table's made from hard plastic, same as the two chairs. We have one window, and I hurry over to get our bearings. The glass is filtered, so we're protected from the sun's rays, and a window shade can be pulled down to shut out the light.

Shoulders touching, J.D. and I stare out at our surroundings. The building we're in is located on a small rise. Below us there are warehouses, a couple of office buildings. Everything looks empty and run-down. There's no fire escape outside our window, no visible way to exit the building except for the way we entered.

"We're well and truly stuck," I say, turning to him with a frown.

"We don't want to get out," he whispers into my ear.

"We don't?"

He shakes his head. "We need to find out what he wants. There's no point in trying to escape 'til we know what it is he's after and how far he's willing to go to get it."

I see his reasoning. "Okay. I'll stay put for now. But I don't trust that guy. Something about him gives me the creeps."

"If it makes you feel any better, I don't think he wants us for dinner," J.D. jokes.

"I refuse to find a bright side to this situation."

"Patience, Kira."

"It's not my best quality."

"I know."

16

He makes us wait two days. For two days, I fret and ponder, pacing the tiny room. After having the whole world to wander, it is torture to be inside, constantly under surveillance. Without freedom, without purpose, I sleep too much. I bicker with J.D. over trivialities, how passively he can stare into space for long stretches of time or the odd habit of lifting his shirt to rub his belly after he eats. Why is this the first time I've noticed this annoying habit? I discover two days is more than enough time to learn every stain and crook and cranny of our small cell.

And yet, I'm not completely uncomfortable.

A sophisticated filtering system has been installed in the building, so we have clean air. We're well fed, and for an hour each day, we're released into a small yard behind the building surrounded by a tall, chain-link fence. Beyond the yard are just more broken-down buildings, as far as the eye can see. Still, it's an hour outside, and we use the time to walk, to do jumping jacks; anything to get our blood pumping. We don't use our facemasks when we go outside. We're only going to be out for a short time. Besides, the air feels, I don't know, it feels okay to me. Or maybe I just don't care anymore whether I'm inhaling toxic air or not.

On the third day, the door opens and the man with the mustache grins at us with casual good humor.

"I hope you two have been comfortable."

I stare at him with cautious disbelief. J.D. and I are prisoners, and he's treating us like we're guests from out-of-town who've spent the last few days taking in the sights.

He shuts the door, pulling over a chair to sit down. He motions for us to do likewise and J.D., and I sit across from him on the bed.

"I apologize for not speaking with you sooner. There's been a lot going on and, naturally, everyone's very excited that you're here."

He might as well be speaking an alien language. Nothing he says makes sense. He looks at me expectantly.

"I don't understand," I say, finally.

"Then I'll explain." He leans forward, placing his elbows on his knees. "We've got machines that can do everything, Kira. We can calculate the most complex equations. We can see and break apart the tiniest atomic particles. We can lift and move anything. Shoot, we can even turn lead into gold. But we've never figured out how to regenerate the natural resources that we've lost."

He sounds earnest and the expression on his face disarms me for a minute, makes me want to trust him. Of course, I know our natural resources weren't *lost*, they were squandered, spoiled, ruined beyond recognition.

"You have a talent, Kira. You tap into something, some universal energy, and you bring forth water. We need that talent."

"Who's 'we?'"

"'We' is the Unified Territories Council, the people who make the hard decisions. We decide who gets water, and who doesn't." Lowering his voice, he holds my gaze meaningfully. "We decide who gets to grow a flower, and who doesn't."

"I didn't grow a flower. It grew by itself."

"But, it couldn't have survived by itself, Kira. It needed you. It needed the water only you can provide."

My head's spinning. I don't want to hear that this man and others like him can cut off people's water supply. Oh, I know that they could, but that they would consider it, that it would even be a topic of discussion in a boardroom somewhere. It's wrong.

"Where do you think the territory gets its water?" he asks, suddenly.

In the past, people had gotten fresh water from glacier mining. But that was before the polar ice melted. "Desalination of the oceans," I tell him.

"That's one way. Of course, the process is not perfect. Transporting fresh water for interior populations creates all kinds of logistical problems. And we're running into issues with the brine residue. No matter how deeply we deposit it back into the oceans, it impacts underwater ecosystems. For the most part, we provide water for the area population to drink—or for agricultural purposes—out of underground reservoirs. But this source is limited, so we have to administer it, with great care and consideration, for the well-being of the entire Territory.

"Because we use hidden sources, we're able to keep a lid on social unrest. People can't get at the water. No one gets more than their fair share. No one knows when our supplies are low or when we're having trouble with toxicity. That's where you come in."

"I don't understand."

"I need you to fill the Opawinge aquifer."

"The Opawinge!"

I try to remember what I learned in school about this underground source. It doesn't exist anymore, but once it had been enormous, stretching beneath three territories. As far as I knew, it had drained out years ago. Now, I wondered. Had that simply been a myth the government wanted us to believe?

"You're delusional," I say shortly, falling back on the one sure reason why it won't work. "I couldn't even fill the lake, which is an open water source, and you're asking me to fill the Opawinge, which covers ten times more area *and* is underground. It's impossible."

"It's not impossible, Kira. I know how to help you. I can help you channel your ability. You *can* do it," he pauses, "with my help."

"I don't want your help." The words are out of my mouth before I can stop them.

He arches one brow but allows my rudeness to pass. "Think for a moment, Kira. Don't let your emotions get the better of you. I'm offering you the chance to save lives. The Council supplies the population with water. Our best and most reliable source is the Opawinge. Currently, we draw out more than 400 million gallons a day to provide water for people's rations, to provide water to area Biospheres. But it's a non-renewable resource. At current draw-down rates, the aquifer will be depleted soon, and more people will die."

A chill passes over me as I listen to Thorne's words. There's no arguing his point. Still, the idea that he can help 'channel' my ability is ridiculous. What does he know about bringing water? I don't even know how I do it, so how could he?

"I've never filled an underground source," I say stubbornly. I don't mention the pool in the cave. Besides, that wasn't an aquifer, so it's not the same thing at all. "I don't even know if it can be done."

"It can be done."

Something in his tone raises the hairs on my arms. He's so absolute. How can he be that certain, unless.... My eyes narrow. "How do you know it can be done?"

"Kira, all those times you called water, didn't you notice that the water goes and stops where you want it? It's like the earth has a memory of water, but it lacks a mental map. It needs you to give it direction, to guide the water where it should go."

He's right. My small ponds and ditches never overflow. They never flood. The water rises, then stops, recognizing some invisible boundary. Do I create that boundary? If he's right, then the same thing would happen in an underground source. The water would fill in the empty spaces of the pattern I create in my mind, like coloring in the outlines of a picture.

"Besides," he says softly, grabbing my attention, "your mother did it."

17

For a moment, if feels like the room and everything in it is far away. A roaring in my ears drowns out my thoughts. My voice, when I finally speak, is raspy. "My mother did this? She called water?"

"She did."

"Are there others?" I whisper.

"Not that we know. Apparently, something happened between your grandmother's generation and your mother's, but she was the first. She came to *me*, Kira. It was a hard time. People were suffering. A lot more people would have died if not for her. She struck a lucrative deal with the Council. She brought water, when and where we needed it. And she was generously rewarded."

I want to disbelieve him. My mother wouldn't be in a partnership with this man, would she? How could I know? How could I trust the things he was telling me? Then again, who else could supply me with answers?

"Tell me about her."

"She was smart and determined;" he says softly, "She understood the value of her talent. She wanted to make a difference in the world. She knew that with the Council's support, she could." Suddenly, his voice trails off. "And she had a perilous beauty."

I focus my gaze on Thorne's face. There's something new in the tone of his voice.

"What was she to you?" I ask, uncertainly.

Slowly, his eyes regain their focus. His look is assessing, scrutinizing. Restless, I jiggle one leg beneath me. J.D. presses his hip against mine to stop the jiggling.

"She was the first to demonstrate a truly miraculous ability," he says. "And it is thanks to me that after your uncle died, a place was found for you at the Garner Home for Girls. We've discovered that not all offspring continue a parent's special ability. In some cases, it does continue, usually after the onset of adolescence, which indicates hormonal development might be involved. In some cases, it mutates into something else. And sometimes, it disappears altogether."

I'm confused. "I thought you said there wasn't anyone else who could make water."

"That's true. You and your mother have been the only ones with that particular gift. But," he shrugs, "let's just say there are other children with interesting potential."

"And you, what? You spy on them?"

"We find them. We place them in special homes. We ensure they receive room and board and a fair education. In return, we ask their caretakers to alert us to any signs of special ability."

Understanding dawns. "And maybe you embed

them with microchips to keep track of them."

He bursts into laughter. "Very good, Kira. Of course, we didn't get to you in time, did we? We'll have to remedy that while you're here."

My mind is overflowing with thoughts and images as I try to make sense of this new information. There are others. Who can do, what? Fly or conjure things out of thin air? My imagination runs wild with the possibilities, although I realize he could mean something much more commonplace. Like little Joey's sense of smell. Maybe there are others who are simply stronger or faster or more resilient in some way.

Glancing at Thorne, I return to the subject of my mother. There are hundreds of things I want to know about the woman who gave birth to me, but I start with the end of the story. "How did she die?"

He doesn't speak for a long moment. Is he deciding whether to tell the truth or a lie? How will I know which he chooses? Finally, he clears his throat.

"She drowned, sadly. For all that she could fill a lake, your mother never learned to swim. She was terrified of water, in fact. She drowned when you were very small."

I can't resist a shiver. I try to take it in, my mind suffused with the image of her and how it must have been: the sinking, the losing of air and memory as the water fills every small part of you. She could fill a lake, but she couldn't empty it. I imagine the helplessness of being surrounded by something of your own creation and then being done in by it. I believe Thorne. I believe he's told me the truth. I realize I don't know anyone who can swim. After all, where would someone learn? Every lake or swimming hole is either dried up or toxic.

"Okay," I say slowly. "I'll help you. I'll try to make water in the Opawinge. I'll give it my best shot, at least. Then J.D. and I can leave. Right?"

"There is the matter of the chip, Kira. We need to be able to locate you, if the need arises. Your talent is vital to the well being of the Territory. But once you've both had microchips embedded, I see no reason why you can't leave."

The idea of having a tracking device embedded beneath my skin turns my stomach. But if it means J.D. and I can leave this place, it will be worth it.

I glance at J.D., but his eyes are noncommittal. Evidently, he's decided this is my decision. Okay then. I nod my head. "I'll need a backpack," I say. "I had one, but I lost it. I want some things."

"Give your list to Michael. He'll take care of it."

After that, things happen quickly. Thorne leaves to prepare for our departure. But as soon as the sun is down, he returns to the room.

"Kira, are you ready?"

"I guess."

J.D. and I both rise, but Thorne shakes his head. "Only you, Kira. There's not space on the chopper. We're going a long way, and we need to keep the craft as light as possible."

J.D.'s gaze is searching on mine. This is unexpected. I can tell he doesn't like it.

"It's okay" I reassure him. "I'll be back in no time."

I'm not sure I believe my own words, but I try not to show it. If necessary, would I try to escape from Thorne if it meant leaving J.D. behind here in Slag? Not likely. I've grown accustomed to his presence. And he didn't leave me behind when I was captured. Maybe Thorne is relying on that, on our loyalty to each other, to keep me obedient. Besides, I'm doing a good thing, I think, in trying to fill the Opawinge. This man, Thorne, knew my mother. She made water for him. I hold onto that thought to give me strength.

I give J.D. a small smile, then follow Thorne out of the room. In a downstairs garage, the armored rover is waiting. From the rover to the chopper takes less than an hour, and then we're darting through the night sky, enveloped in blackness.

I'm finding it hard to breathe. This is my first time ever in the air. And already, I miss J.D.; I'm not used to being without him. What if Thorne doesn't bring me back? I push down an edge of panic. I don't need this now. A small flutter like moth wings begins to beat beneath my left eyelid. I press my hand against my eye to stop the tic, then sigh when the fluttering moves to my other eye.

The Opawinge—what am I thinking? I don't care what Thorne says. If I couldn't fill the lake, then an underground reservoir is way out of my league. Then again, to be able to do it, to do something that would save lives, would be amazing. And what if I can't fill it? What will Thorne do?

After a moment, I realize he's staring at me.

"What?"

"Even if you had filled the lake," he says thoughtfully, "did it occur to you that the whole area is toxic?"

"I know the area's toxic. I figured the water would help. It cleans things."

"Sometimes. However, most toxic contaminants are persistent. It's essential that each aquatic ecosystem be restored in an orderly and systematic fashion."

I stare at him blankly.

"Where are the fish in your lake?" he continues.

"Well..." I'm puzzled by his question. Its very obviousness is annoying. "...someone would have to put them in."

"Let's say, for the moment, that it's a possibility. That we have fish in an aquarium somewhere that only need a new home to be happy and begin making happy fish babies, so we deposit them in your lake. What would they eat?"

I don't want to answer his questions. I glance out the window, gazing blindly at the distant twinkling of stars. "That's not my problem."

"No, it's mine. Restoration is a holistic process, Kira, not achieved through the isolated manipulation of individual elements. Merely recreating a form without the functions does not constitute restoration. There has to be life, fish and native plants to keep the water oxygenated. There has to be a chemical adjustment of the soil and the water and the area toxins."

"I just bring the water," I say stubbornly, annoyed.

"Of course you do, dear. Quite right."

I hate his smug tone and his big words and how on earth am I supposed to know about "aquatic ecosystems" anyway? I'm relieved when he pulls out a computer and begins to work. I curl in my seat and close my eyes. If a person knows how to do something and do it well, then it would be wrong not to do that thing, right? I mean, if it's a good thing, if it causes no harm. I make water. It's what I do. The fish and all that other stuff, someone else can be responsible for it. The fish can't come until the water's there anyway.

When I wake up, the sun is rising. Light leaks in between cracks in the chopper's sun filters, and I shield my eyes from the glare, reaching into my pack to retrieve new eyeshades.

"We're here," Thorne says softly.

In minutes, we're landing, kicking up a swirl of dust in an area that appears completely desolate. There's nothing as far as the eye can see except sand and grit and sheer white air. We unload our bags then roar off in another rover. I turn to Thorne. "I've been thinking about what you said."

"What did I say?"

"All that stuff about toxins being in the lake. In school, I was taught that the Opawinge was ruined. So why fill it if the water's going to be unfit?"

"You're thinking, Kira. That's good. It *is* possible to clean aquifers of volatile organic compounds. However, it's costly and time-consuming. Naturally, toxins need to be eliminated before we try to turn any site into a functioning water source for human consumption."

"Then, it would be possible to clean the Dead Lakes area, too," I ask.

"Theoretically."

I digest this information. If Thorne really can help me channel this ability, then eventually I could still fill the lake. And it could be cleaned and someone could plant the seeds of green things and put fish in the water. I slide a gaze to the man beside me. "In other words, the aquifer's clean?"

"The Opawinge receives regular maintenance. During the years right after your mother filled it, we removed trichloroethene and 1,1-dichloroethene, as well as volatile and semivolatile hydrocarbons using *in situ* ground water remediation technology."

I yawn dramatically, ignoring a sudden bark of laughter from Thorne.

The rover takes us through miles of desert. Invisible until we're right upon it, a hole opens up in the ground and soon we're heading downhill into a subterranean passage. The darkness is a relief from the harsh sun and I remove my shades, letting my eyes adjust, taking in the cavernous walls of the tunnel.

When we stop, we're poised on a stone platform. Stepping out of the rover, I'm immediately assaulted by the scent of water. Even though I know I'm directly below the desert sand, here there is moisture. It seeps from the walls and forms a small pool below the platform, then snakes behind walls of rock and I can't tell how far it goes or how deep.

I look up at Thorne. "What now?"

"I want you right by the water, Kira. Touch it. Sink your hands into the pool."

I've only ever filled areas that were dry on their surface, with no residual moisture that I could detect. This feels odd, to be making water while surrounded by evidence of it.

"Close your eyes."

I do what he asks. I slip my hands into the water, and it's cold and slick. I give an involuntary shiver, then take a deep breath and release it, closing my eyes.

"You've studied the diagrams of the aquifer that I gave to you, correct?"

"Yes."

"Picture what lies beyond these walls of rock and sand, Kira. The water underground is not like a river or a lake. Sometimes it's a layer, in between the hardness above and below it. Sometimes, the water is a trickle snaking along a labyrinth of tiny passages in permeable rock, worn through by ten million years of constant seeping. And sometimes it's a saturated layer of gravel and sand and clay.

"Right now, you're standing at the brink of a quarter million square miles of aquifer. This space used to contain not just millions of gallons but millions of billions of gallons of water. Picture all of it. Picture it empty, missing the water that was there before. And you can take away the emptiness. Take it away, Kira. Bring the water level up. Fill the pools and the passages. Open your mind and let your thoughts flow. The water will flow with them."

121

Thorne's words are softly spoken. His even tone sends me into an altered state where I feel invisible to myself. If I'm tangible at all, it's as a slight damp thing, a rag being twisted to wring from it every last molecule of moisture.

Condensation on the platform has seeped into my clothes. I'm cold and trembling when I open my eyes and look up at him.

He places his hand gently on my shoulder. "Wish for the water, Kira. Wish for it now."

I gaze up at this man, who suddenly seems like a comfort in this dark place. He knew my mother. And maybe he understands what I want to do, who I want to be. I hear him mumbling softly, his own water wish perhaps? *"Speak ye unto the rock and there shall come water out of it, that the people may drink..."* He closes his eyes, but keeps his hand on my shoulder.

"I wish for water," I whisper, my teeth chattering on the words. "I wish for water to fill up this place."

18

"J.D! We're back!" I bound up the stairs, my pack forgotten on the landing below. J.D. hears me coming and steps out of the room in time for me to knock him over in a move that's part tackle, part hug. "We're back!"

I can't believe how happy I feel. When was the last time I felt like this? Have I ever? Surprised, J.D. catches the tackle and manages to stumble backwards without falling over and hurting either one of us. "How'd it go?"

I release him and bounce over to the bed. "It was good. It was really good. Different than anything I've ever done before."

"Tell me."

"We went underground in the desert, and there was some water, of course, but you could tell that this huge cavernous place used to be just full of it. I could feel the presence of the water, J.D. It wasn't just that there was moisture on the walls and that damp smell and all of that. I mean, I could *feel* it in my bones, the moisture, the memory of it, in that place. That's never happened to me before. And Thorne helped."

"He *what*?" The look on his face is comical.

"Oh, he couldn't physically help, of course. But he seems to get it, you know. What it takes, how it feels. He talked me through the whole thing."

He looks suspicious. "And it worked? You were able to make the water?"

"Sure. I mean," I falter, "I guess so."

"You *guess* so?"

"Well, I didn't actually see that it had worked," I say slowly. "The Opawinge's not like something you can just see fill up, like a pond. But Thorne took a few readings the next day and said we could leave. So, I assumed ... ."

"But he didn't actually confirm that you'd filled the aquifer?"

"Geez, J.D. What's your problem?" I march to the window then turn to glare at him. He's spoiling my mood. It's been so long since I felt happy. I want to hold onto it. "Don't you think we'd have stayed there longer if I *hadn't* done it? I thought you'd be glad for me—for us. Now that I filled the Opawinge, we can go. I can try the lake again. I'm sure I can do it this time. "

"Great. Fine. Fantastic. When can we leave?"

"Soon, I think," I tell him, my mind going to the procedure that must be performed first. "Once the chips are in, you know, so Thorne can find us if he needs us."

He frowns at me, stuffing his hands in his pockets. "Wow. What happened to Kira? I think Thorne left with one person and brought back another. You've sure changed your tune."

I'm not going to let him needle me. I'm not. I'll count. That's it. I'll count to ten before I respond. One, two, three.... "I think it's important that I be available, J.D. Thorne needs to be able to locate me when the territory needs water is all." I take a deep breath. I'm sure once J.D. understands, it'll be fine. "It's not like just anybody can do this, you know. And the Territory's need for water—it's not going to go away. The chip means freedom. We can travel wherever we want, but if the Territory needs me, then.... Besides, the chip insertion is just a tiny prick. Thorne says it won't hurt a bit."

"Thorne, Thorne, Thorne."

I press my hands together, resisting the urge to ball them into fists and sock him. "I don't know why you've got this bug up your butt, J.D. It's not like you've been suffering here. You get three meals a day, a bed to sleep in each night. And Thorne's trying to make a difference. He's trying to help me. He thinks what I can do is important."

"Of course it's important!" he shouts, startling me. "What you can do is amazing. But is he really trying to help you, Kira? From where I stand, it looks like you're the only one doing any helping around here. We're still his prisoners, you know."

"I'm sure we can leave soon."

"Not so fast, Kira," says Thorne, stepping into the room. "I need you here a little longer."

I send him a confused glance. "I don't understand. I mean, it worked, didn't it? I filled the Opawinge?"

"No." His tone is somber. "I'm sorry. It didn't work."

"But...." I don't know how to absorb it, the sudden breathtaking sense of failure. I lean against the wall, one

125

hand pressing against the sick feeling roiling in my belly. Why must my emotions always go straight to my stomach? I glare up at Thorne. "If I didn't do it, why didn't you let me try again? I thought..." I gaze at J.D. in dismay and embarrassment. He must think I'm a total idiot. I turn back to Thorne. "You should have told me. You should have told me right away. If I'd had more time...."

"It was evident to me that you weren't ready, Kira. That's why we left. There's a barrier you haven't crossed yet. Perhaps because you're still young. It's like any other talent. You need to develop it. You need to practice on smaller, more manageable efforts."

"I've done that!"

"I can work with you. I can help you," he says, his tone soothing. "Then, when you're ready, we'll go back. We'll make it work."

I can't believe it didn't work. I whirl and smack the wall, wincing as the pain shoots up my arm. It felt like it worked. It felt inside like I had the power to make it happen. I turn and glance at J.D. His eyes are wary, guarded. Suddenly, I've got to get out of here.

"I left my pack downstairs," I say shortly. "I'm going to get it."

When Thorne came upstairs, he must have dismissed the guard, because there's no one in the hallway to witness my dash from the room. I reach the first floor, and my pack is resting on a hall table. The door leading outside is ajar, and I step forward. Maybe I can get away for a bit. I want to wander the streets until I shake off this funk, this awful feeling that I've lost it. I've lost the only thing that made me special in the world.

Before I can step outside, Thorne's voice stops me.

"You *can* do it, Kira," he says softly. "You felt it at the Opawinge, didn't you? You felt that power inside you."

Slowly, I turn and face him. This man knew my mother. Perhaps he even had feelings for her. And he wants to help me. He's going to help me learn how to use my gift so people can be saved. That's what's important. I mustn't be impatient. That's always my problem. I take a deep breath and try to answer him honestly.

"I thought I did. I felt...something." I shrug. "Maybe it was only my imagination."

He shakes his head. "It wasn't your imagination. You're very close. You're going to make it happen, Kira." He gestures up the stairs. "Now, why don't you spend some time with J.D.? I'm sure he missed you."

I resist the urge to roll my eyes. He certainly hadn't acted like he missed me. "Yeah," I mutter finally, glancing back at the door to the outside, to freedom. "Sure." I take my pack from the table and head upstairs.

When I get to the room, it's empty. "J.D.?" I drop my pack on the bed and step back into the hall. "J.D.?" There's no answer. That's odd. Where'd he go?

"It's up!"

I jump when J.D. grabs my shoulder, his voice whispering urgently into my ear. I send him a baffled glance. "What are you talking about?"

"The water! The lake! It's up!" He takes my hand and drags me toward the stairs. "Thorne didn't want you to know. He wanted you to doubt yourself. I don't know why, Kira. Maybe he wanted you off balance so he could control you. He wanted you to think you needed him. But you don't. You don't have to doubt yourself. It took some time, that's all. It didn't fill in a rush or a flood—maybe it was just a trickle—but it *did* fill."

I clamber behind him as he pulls me up flights of stairs, my mind trying to grasp the full import of what he's saying. Is it possible? No. Surely not.

"There was just something about Thorne," he says. His voice is low, but insistent. "You were so sure you'd filled the Opawinge, and I believed you. Then Thorne gave us all that stuff about you not being ready. It didn't feel right, not when you'd been so certain. I've never seen you so exuberant, so sure of yourself. Don't forget, I've seen what you can do. So, when he left to look for you, I decided to investigate."

On the top floor, J.D. steers me into a richly paneled room and turns me toward the window.

"Look. There. Between those two buildings. See?"

I look where he's pointing; desperate to see what he believes is there.

"I don't see anything."

"It's blue. There's a shimmer just above the water. Look into the distance."

I look, and look again. I squint and scan. And then, I see it. Between a crack in the city skyline, there's a slice of blue. I inhale a sharp breath. J.D.'s right. The lake is full.

19

"I did it," I whisper numbly.

J.D. turns me by the shoulders and gives me a slight shake. "We have to get out of here, Kira. Can't you see what's going on? He doesn't want you to know because he doesn't want you to leave. Ever."

My hands are shaking. I hear the words, but it's like something's gummed up the works. My brain can't process them correctly. Slowly, it starts to sink in—I did make the water. The lake is full, and Thorne's been lying to us, to me, the whole time.

"Take the boy."

Thorne's voice is flat, freezing the room for a split second before things break loose. A guard rushes into the room. I move to block J.D., but I'm not fast enough. The guard lifts me out of the way like I was a sack of beans while another one of Thorne's henchmen twists J.D.'s arm behind his back. In a flash, J.D. back-kicks the man's knee with a sickening crunch, bringing him to his knees. Then he runs at my guard, who drops me and advances to meet J.D. with a right hook to his jaw.

J.D. dodges the blow.

"Get out, Kira!"

I dart toward the door, ducking as Thorne reaches for me. His hand misses my collar but manages to grab hold of the hair at the back of my head. He wrenches his arm back, jerking me off my feet. I yelp with the pain, my hands reaching behind me to claw at Thorne's wrists.

By now, two more guards have entered, grabbing J.D. and knocking him out cold. They carry him from the room, while I kick and struggle, cracking the back of my head against Thorne's face. It feels good to hurt him. He swears and crushes me so tightly I think I feel a rib crack. With a jerk, he tosses me across the room. I collapse against the wall. Quickly, I try to figure the best way to launch a new attack. Where are they taking J.D.? I have to get to him. Thorne sees my intention and steps between me and the door, blocking my exit. The man with the soothing voice who coaxed me to believe in myself has disappeared.

"You lied to me," I say bitterly.

"Kira, listen to me. I had good reason."

"I did fill the Opawinge, didn't I?"

He nods. "It's not full, yet. But, the water level is rising. It will be full by the end of the week."

"Then I did what you asked. I refilled the Opawinge. I'm done now. You promised to let us go."

He sighs, rubbing his hand over his face. "Like you said, I lied."

"Why?"

"I need you too much," he says. "The Territory needs

you too much. I don't want to hurt you. I don't want to hurt J.D. But this is bigger than one person. Try to understand. I'm trying to save an entire planet."

"But I want to save the planet, too. We want the same thing."

He folds his arms and leans against the wall tiredly. "I'd love to let you go, but I can't. I can't risk something happening to you. It's a dangerous world out there. And it's my job to manage natural resources. Like it or not, Kira, you're a natural resource."

"What are you afraid of," I sneer, "that if you leave me unattended for even a minute, I'll report you to the authorities?"

He gives me a weary smile. "Report me to whom, Kira? I already act on the highest authority. There's no one for you to report me to and no one who would care if you did."

I believe him. He has all the power here. All I have is my ability to make water. How can I leverage that to help J.D.?

Reluctantly, I change my tone. Maybe conciliation will work where threats won't. "If you let me go, I can make lots of water, Thorne. I can fill rivers and lakes and I know they won't be clean and everything, but you'll clean them, and you'll put in the stuff they need to be living water systems. With my help, you can fix things."

He regards me solemnly. "With your help, I *am* going to fix things."

I shake my head, pressing one hand to my side. "I don't understand."

"It's delicate, Kira. I don't expect you to understand. Believe me, the welfare of the Territories is my first concern, but there's a process which must be followed. A fragile balance of power and resources must be maintained. We don't want to recreate another situation of having unregulated population growth. Right now, the population continues to dwindle, and we help regulate that with our distribution of resources. It's unclear yet how the rapid rate of mutations will affect civilization. I assume, at some point, our population will reach stasis. We'll become balanced at a sustainable level. The genetically strong will be all that are left, an accelerated demonstration of survival of the fittest." He steps away from the wall. "That's when we'll rebuild in earnest, Kira. And yes, you will be a vital part of that development. You'll make water strategically, when and where it's most needed."

I stare at him in horror. He's talking about a lifetime of servitude. There's no telling how long it could take for him to fulfill his plans. When we were on the chopper headed to the Opawinge, I'd gotten the idea that he cared about the land and the water and the people who depended upon it. And for a minute in the aquifer, I'd even gotten the impression that he cared about me. Stupid, stupid girl. Now everything's all mixed up. Everything seems to depend upon a political agenda I can't comprehend.

"It's wrong to ration the water if I—if we—can make plenty of it. People's lives matter," I say finally, finding my voice.

"People's lives matter to them. But in the big picture, some people's lives matter more than others. That's just the way it is and always has been. Every species has a pecking order, a hierarchy. Human beings are no different. You're sentimental because you're young. But water's a commodity. And when it's scarce, it becomes valuable currency. It's important to ensure that the strongest and most deserving have their needs met first. It's how we help the population and the planet achieve balance during this delicate period. The Council determines who gets their ration, who doesn't, and who gets a little extra for good behavior. Soon, as this phase of evolution has played itself out, we'll have a clearer picture of what our future resource needs will be."

"But evolution takes centuries. What can you do in one lifetime?"

"Evolution can be shaped and encouraged, if you know what you're doing. And history has shown us that there are occasional leaps, sudden appearances of something new and unexpected in the genetic soup. In just the last three generations, we've seen remarkable transitions. It was the fallout from the Devastation that did it. New chemicals or viruses entering our body and interacting with something. I'm not sure what. We're still trying to figure it out—something smaller and more fundamental to life than even DNA. Your ability to call forth water is just one example of how the universe is responding to this challenge."

He pushes himself away from the wall. "We may not understand it all just yet. But the best scientific minds are working on it. This is a dangerous time we're living in, Kira, but it's also a time of exciting possibility."

"Not for most people. Not everyone feels a sense of possibility. For most people it's only a question of how many days or weeks or months they can survive."

"Yes. And that's unfortunate. But not everyone will succumb to an early death, Kira. Some inhabitants will adapt to the new toxins in our environment. At the cellular level, people are changing into something different. Soon, human achievement will be nurtured again and individuals with beneficial mutations will be protected. People like you."

"But to take away people's water..." I mutter numbly.

"We don't 'take it away,' Kira. Circumstances have done that. We moderate the distribution of what's left. That's all. And we'll moderate the distribution of what you produce. It's how we maintain order. The rules and the rationing actually help people to feel safe, to feel looked after in this big, scary world."

"You're deluded. Who do you know who feels safe?"

"Compared to where we've been, people *are* safer. There's less ambiguity, you see, about what life has in store for them. And it's been years since there was any threat of imminent attack from our enemies, because people in every part of the world are simply too busy trying to survive to the next day. People don't have time to get into trouble when they're thirsty. They can't make war. They don't have the energy for petty squabbles or to kill or steal for political gain..."

I consider the bandits who'd captured me. "But

they'll kill to survive. And if they're thirsty enough, they'll steal the water."

"But they can't, Kira. We control all the clean water, or at least we did until you got it into your head to fill the Dead Lakes. The Lakes are, indeed, a very big target for anyone insane enough to try and take control of it. Naturally, we're already moving to control that situation. It's to our advantage that this area's largely uninhabited. It gives us time to put a plan into place before word spreads and people begin to flock here. We've posted toxic warning signs around the perimeter of the lake and we've started spreading various rumors to account for the sudden appearance of the water. Most people are sheep, Kira, deep down. They're followers. They want someone to tell them what to do. And don't forget the universal fear of anything out of the ordinary."

"They might be afraid at first, until they realize there's nothing to fear. They'll drink the water, and when nothing happens, they'll know it's safe."

"But something *will* happen, Kira," Thorne says softly. "They'll drink the water, and they'll die. If not on their own from natural causes then with a little help. All it takes are a few deaths and the rumors and the fears will grow. It's unfortunate that some have to die, but in the long run, it will protect our ability to control the population, which is in everybody's best interests."

His voice is so calm, so rational. I want to scream with frustration. I can feel the thin thread of control I've been clinging to unraveling. There's something terribly wrong here. Maybe it's true that sometimes lives have

135

to be sacrificed for a greater cause. I'm not sure. But where's the good in this? Thorne's way can't be right.

"Eventually, we'll funnel the water we need to sanitation facilities for cleaning and storage," he continues. "The fact that the lake has water again is just a glitch we'll turn to our advantage. It changes nothing. We still control the source and the distribution of the territory's water."

"You don't control me." I snap.

He turns casually and moves to a control panel on the wall. One touch of his hand has a section of the wall sliding back to reveal a communications switchboard and screen. "Don't I?"

With a press of a button, the screen comes to life. I move closer, my fingers twitching. On the screen I can see J.D., curled into a fetal position on the floor of a bare room. There's blood smeared on his cheek. He's not moving.

20

Back in my room, limbs tremble and fingers clatter clumsily as I reach for the bedrail and miss, stumbling dizzily. I'm suddenly aware of fragility. My own and J.D.'s. I'm not equipped to deal with this situation. I don't know what to do. How am I going to save myself? How am I going to save J.D.?

I gaze unseeing out the window. Absently, I'm aware that evening is sliding over the city. Darkness creeps across roads and buildings. And it's creeping inside me, too. No matter how hard I think, I can come up with only one idea. I'll have to work for Thorne and the Territory Council for the rest of my life. I'll make water when and where he directs. Isn't that what my mother did? And in return for my compliance, he'll have to let J.D. go free. But he'll be free without me by his side. I'm unable to hold back a low whimper. A stab of pain in my gut has me clutching the bed. I inhale slowly through my nose and exhale through my mouth. Inhale. Exhale. After a minute, the pain subsides.

Of course, Thorne is a liar. Once you know a man is a liar, he can't be counted on to tell the truth about anything. *Anything.* Carefully, I stand on shaky legs and begin to pace the small confines of the room, turning my eyes away from the sight of J.D.'s empty bed. How many nights have I fallen asleep listening to his gentle snore? His small slices of breath in the night are familiar and comforting. I have a sudden memory of his hands. I like his hands. I like the way his slender fingers move expertly over equipment or hurl stones with startling accuracy. My observations of him feel like tiny secrets. But I'm not the observant one, not really. It is J.D. who watches things. He watches everything. He pays attention. Not like me. I'm always the oblivious one. *Think, Kira, think.*

I hear a tray of food being placed outside my door. When did I eat last? I had nuts and dried fruit on the chopper. That was a lifetime ago, but it doesn't matter. Nothing matters but saving J.D..

It's almost dawn when I collapse with exhaustion onto the bed. My eyes are drifting shut when I remember the fortune-teller's words. *In the world there is nothing more submissive and weak than water. Yet for attacking that which is hard and strong, nothing can surpass it.*

My eyes flicker open, but I remain still, considering the cryptic message. Was there an answer here? Could my ability to make water save J.D.? As I lay in the dark, trembling, I glimpse something—a whisper of an idea. Like a small seed, it takes root and begins to grow. It's a wild thought, but it just might work. I will have to be very, very patient. And that will be very, very hard.

When Thorne enters my room the next day, I'm

138

ready. I sit, composed and dry-eyed, on one of the plastic chairs by the window.

"You're looking well this morning," he says. His eyes bore into mine, trying to penetrate my thoughts. I guess his intentions and shield myself from his probing, keeping my face carefully blank.

"You win," I say softly. I'm quiet for a moment, not because I'm unsure of what I have to say, but because I want to make sure Thorne is listening. Even if he doubts my next words, there has to be a part of him willing to believe I'm sincere. "A long time ago, my mother made a deal with you, right?"

"That's correct."

"Now, you and I will make a deal. From now on, I work for you. I make water whenever and wherever you require. In return, you let J.D. go free."

He purses his lips, considering my offer. "Not free, Kira," he says. "He's a resourceful lad. He might try to kidnap you for his own purposes."

"Don't be ridiculous. J.D. doesn't need me for any purpose."

"Yes, of course, you'd like to believe that. But really, Kira, think about it. Deep in his heart, J.D. is a loner. Why is a loner, a troublemaker, someone who's spent his entire childhood getting into scrapes with the law, suddenly traveling around the territories with a mutant girl? Out of the goodness of his heart? I've done my research. I think I understand J.D. better than you do."

Why is he saying this to me? Why does he want me to doubt J.D.? And yet, my stomach lurches dangerously.

Perhaps Thorne has a point. Not for the first time, I wonder why J.D. has stayed with me, walked by my side all the way to Slag. Stop it, Kira! I push the thought away. It's more of Thorne's deception. I need to focus on what I know to be real. Remember, Thorne never does anything without a hidden agenda.

"J.D. is my friend." I say the words to Thorne then repeat them silently to myself. And I believe them. J.D. is my friend. And I am his. "If you want me to work for you, if you want me easy-to-get-along-with, then at least let him come back here, back to the room with me."

"I don't trust him."

"And I don't trust you, but we have to start somewhere. I'll talk to J.D. I'll make sure he doesn't cause you any trouble. But your guards have to get off our backs. No more manhandling and spying on us and lurking outside the door. Agreed?"

He studies me for a moment. "It would be naïve of me to believe you, Kira, and I have never been naïve in my life. But to the degree that you're willing to cooperate with me, I'll release J.D., and the two of you may continue to stay here as my guests."

"As your prisoners," I whisper. I'm tired of deception.

"Under my protection," he amends firmly. "I *am* trying to do good work here, Kira, although I know you can't see that yet. Perhaps when you're older, this will make sense to you. In the meantime, I'll improve your accommodations and see that you lack for nothing. You and J.D. will have chips embedded, of course, so we can keep track of your whereabouts. You'll make water at my direction. In time, based upon how well you do, your freedoms may be expanded. You may even come to enjoy the life I can offer you. Do we have a deal?"

I walk over to him and hold out my hand. He takes it, and we exchange a brief, but binding, handshake. "Deal," I whisper, the word choking in my throat.

J.D. returns to the room minutes later, sullen and quiet. His face is swollen and purple bruises line his arms and shoulders. I'm filled with a rage deeper than anything I've ever experienced. I can feel something cracking inside me, a blackness splintering into shards of glacial hatred directed at one man. If Thorne could see this glittering iciness inside me, I think that he would be afraid. For a moment, I'm afraid of myself.

"Are you okay?" I whisper.

"I'm fine."

"Can I get you anything?"

"I'm fine, Kira. It's not like I've never taken a punch before. I got a few licks in myself, you know," he says, eyes flashing. "But I've had it with Thorne. I'm out of here, whether you're coming with me or not."

"Of course, I'm coming with you, J.D." I resist the urge to reach out in reassurance. "Believe me; I don't want to stay here anymore than you do."

"Well," he gazes at me warily. "I wasn't sure."

"Actually, I've been thinking of a way. I've just got to think on it a little more."

With difficulty, he lowers himself onto his bed. "That's good, then. We'll go over everything later. Right now, I'm going to rest." He stretches out slowly, wincing as his body shifts to find a comfortable position. In minutes, he's asleep.

Gently, I pull the sheet over his shoulders.

For the next few days, Thorne's men watch us closely, but they leave us alone. J.D. is stiff and sore, so I request a reading device and some downloads. I pass the time reading, sometimes to myself; sometimes aloud, whenever I come across something I think he might find interesting.

Thorne is nowhere in sight. I assume the sudden appearance of water in the Dead Lakes has caused him all kinds of headaches. If so, I'm glad of it. Still, I worry he'll put something into the water to make people sick. Was he being serious when he said people would have to die if they drank the water? Of course, he was, I tell myself crossly. Why do I still want to believe there's good in this man?

Even though J.D. isn't up to strenuous exercise, I never fail to take my hour outdoors. I've stepped up my exercising, but not too noticeably. I don't want the guards to get suspicious. When I'm outside, I jump rope then jog laps around the perimeter of the yard. When I don't have any wind left, I find a place in the shade near the back wall of the building and lie down as though I'm simply trying to catch my breath. Is it my imagination or is the air cleaner, fresher? Could water in the lake make a difference this quickly? I can't see vapor coming off the water, of course, but I can imagine its evaporation slowly working to create change in the air we breathe.

Maybe it is the crispness of the air that keeps me

energized. Later, when I'm back in our room with the door closed, I do push-ups and sit-ups until I'm limp.

"Why the heavy workout?" J.D. asks.

"Because when we get out of here, I want to be ready. I want to be strong."

His eyes narrow, assessing me. Then, he joins me on the floor.

"Hold my feet," he says shortly.

I sit across his feet and wrap my arms around his calves, holding him as he begins his sit-ups. "One, two, three..."

After that, J.D. goes outside with me every day. He chats with the guards. He's better at that than I am. The same men who hurt him, he now treats as though they were old friends. He thinks up jokes and teases them, but not in a way to get them riled up, only to show there are no hard feelings.

And he exercises with me. Gradually, we're rebuilding our muscles, increasing our stamina to the point where we'll be able to walk again, away from this place.

We end each session outdoors by collapsing by the back corner of the building. To the guards, it looks as though we're worn out from exercise and taking a rest. J.D. blocks me from view as I direct my attention to the ground and wish for water.

"Did you know once upon a time, this whole area was covered by water?" I whisper.

"It must have been a long time ago."

"The memory of water is here, J.D. The question is, do I have any control at all over where it goes?"

143

"And if this doesn't work?"

"It's got to work. Right now, the dirt beneath this building is dry and stable, but water is a terrific lubricant. If I can just make the water *here*, then everything beneath the foundation will shift."

"At least we have a good slope."

"It could be better. If we were on higher ground, we'd really have gravity on our side." I glance around, wrinkling my nose at the gentle slope of land away from the building. What I wouldn't give right now for a steep incline and potential mudslide. "This will have to do."

One of the guards shouts that our time is up and we stand, dusting off our britches. As we head inside, I force myself not to look back at the wall. I know there's nothing there, no stain on the ground, no newly formed cracks in the mortar. So far, I've been completely ineffectual.

That night, after a meal of deep fried crickets with ginger sauce, J.D. and I lie in our beds talking quietly.

"Once Thorne returns, he's going to have chips embedded," he reminds me. "If something doesn't happen soon, it won't matter. He'll be able to track us wherever we go."

"We *will* get away, J.D. I'll cut the chip out of myself if I have to," I insist. "Or we'll cut them out of each other."

He nods his agreement.

"Can I ask you a question?" I whisper.

"If you're asking permission, it must be important."

"What does J.D. stand for?"

He's silent for a long time, and I'm worried he'll give me another smug answer. I couldn't stand that, not now, not after all we've been through together. "I don't have a mother or father," he begins slowly, "none that ever acknowledged me. And DNA testing isn't exactly accurate when everyone's carrying around chromosomal anomalies."

I get it now. "You're one of the John Doe babies."

John Doe. J.D.

Immediately after the Devastation, when chaos reigned and masses of people died daily from poisons of one sort or another, thousands of babies were abandoned. Maybe their parents were dying, maybe they were indifferent. Maybe they no longer saw the point of bringing life into a world that seemed determined to extinguish it. The babies who were found before they died were gathered into institutions. Most didn't survive. They were the John Does and the Jane Does. The left behind, the unwanted.

"I believe you," I say softly. "Thank you."

My eyelids are getting heavy and my mind's starting to wander when I speak again. "Do you think Tamara and Shay are alright?" I whisper. I've never asked Thorne about them. At first, I was afraid he'd tell me they'd been interrogated at Bio-4. But now I realize every person I care about is one more person Thorne can use to manipulate me. If he knew how much they meant to me, they'd be in danger. So, I can't mention their names to him, ever.

"I don't see what purpose it'd serve by harming

them," J.D. says finally. "Thorne is, above all, a practical man."

"True."

For awhile, we're quiet, lost in our own thoughts. Then, J.D.'s voice, soft and low, floats across the room.

"I answered your question. Answer one of mine."

"Okay."

"It's silly."

"I don't mind."

"If eternity had a sound, what would it be?"

I'm quiet for a minute, imagining eternity. I remember a picture I saw in a book once, a ladder curving up through clouds and clusters of angels. Images come to mind like infinite space and infinite darkness, but a sound? The haunting notes of an oboe dance lightly on the edges of consciousness, pulling me forward through imaginary soundscapes. Finally, it comes to me. "Eternity is the sound the ocean makes," I say drowsily, before drifting into sleep.

21

Matron once told me that volcanoes, right before they erupt, emit a tone, a long, slow wail that can only be heard by the most sensitive scientific equipment. I've always wondered if that was the earth's way of warning inhabitants of the destruction to come or if it was a song, a celebration of nature's terrible, destructive majesty.

Deep in sleep, surrounded by darkness, my eyes fly open, and I sit bolt upright in bed. There's a whine in the air, a groan, and then I feel a shift beneath my bed.

"Kira!"

The floor hitches once more, and I clamber up and grab hold of the headboard.

"Don't just sit there," J.D. barks from across the room. "Move!"

I turn my head, eyes straining foggily to focus. "What's happening?"

"Get your shoes, quick!" he whispers. "Grab your pack."

"Now?"

"Now!"

Hurriedly, I grab my shoes and my gear, making sure my bedroll is tied securely to my pack. I sense movement, below and a light's been turned on somewhere, its glow seeping beneath the locked door of our room. I hear a shout downstairs.

Suddenly, there's a huge cracking sound and our room tilts. Both beds crash into the far wall, and we're unable to prevent ourselves from tumbling after them.

"Hang on!" I shout, as everything begins to move. There's a violent ripping and tearing from both above and below us, and then we're falling. J.D. and I reach for each other, fighting to keep the chairs from landing on our heads as the whole structure around us suddenly drops, then pitches forward.

There's crashing and a splintering of wood and concrete and plaster, and we're rolling, stumbling against one wall, then another. Then we're on the ground and rolling as fast as we can to get out of the way of falling debris.

"Watch out!" J.D. yells, veering aside into dark wet dirt and grabbing hold. I'm beside him, covered in mud and dust and trying to dig my fingers into the soil deeply enough to gain purchase. The ground all around us has opened up into a giant crater. One half of the building has collapsed into the hole, beams snapped like matchsticks, and bricks seared apart along jagged edges of mortar.

"It's the Granddaddy of all sinkholes!" exults J.D.

I turn to look at him, and he's unrecognizable. Covered head to toe in mud, he looks like a swamp creature. The whites of his eyes are all that's visible in the darkness. Hearing voices, I glance up to see interior lights flickering inside what's left of our prison, along with shouts from the guards. The building has been sheared in half and wires and pipes dangle loosely from exposed rooms.

Suddenly Thorne steps into view on what is left of the third floor. His body is backlit, but even with his face in the darkness, I can tell he's taut with rage.

"Kira!" he shouts. "You can't get away, Kira!"

It's dark in the hole, and I'm certain he can't see us, but it feels as though he's looking right at me. His voice carries easily in the night air.

"Think about this, Kira, before you do anything drastic. Your mother tried to leave, too. She didn't make it."

I'm shivering uncontrollably, frozen with fear in the mud and the muck. Did she drown trying to get away from Thorne, then? It doesn't even occur to me that he might have killed her. His plans wouldn't allow him to destroy the one person who could serve his ambition.

I glance up as a new creaking reaches my ears, a groaning caused by additional strain on the foundation. The remaining half of the building shifts, jolting Thorne sideways. He crashes into a wall. Slipping, he grabs hold of a floorboard for support. His body dangles a moment, poised over the sinkhole, and I see him grasping with his other hand to find something he can use for leverage.

The building convulses once again, shaking loose his grip. I watch as he falls, his body striking the side of the hole, then rolling to the bottom. My eyes strain in the darkness, waiting to see a movement among the piles of debris.

"Come on, Kira," J.D. whispers urgently. "We've got to get out of here. Give me your hand."

He reaches for me, and I grab hold, letting him pull me behind him up the wall of mud. Soon, we reach what appears to be a more stable area, and I follow him quietly as we clamber over cinderblocks and pieces of furniture and out of the sinkhole. Casting a last look back, I see guards rushing outside, shining flashlights into the wreckage below. It's an unreal scene, like the fuzzy black and white images pulled from an old newsreel of a natural disaster. I smile coldly into the dark pit, silently wishing Thorne the worst. Then stepping through the torn fence, I launch into a trot beside J.D.

We set a quick pace, not stopping for anything. All is quiet, but we know it's just a matter of time before a search party begins tracking us. I know they'll use choppers and surveillance equipment, and we'll need to be hidden before daybreak.

I think about Thorne's last words then quickly swallow the slippery fear inching its way toward my heart. My mother might have died trying to get away from him, but that doesn't mean it wasn't worth the effort. It doesn't mean J.D. and I can't make it happen. And if Thorne died in the fall, then who'll come after us? Will anyone still care? I don't know. But my gut instinct tells me he's not dead. If we survived, so could he. But he might be slowed down. If we're lucky, it'll be enough.

Turning a corner, we suddenly find ourselves on Lake Shore Drive, and we pause to take in the scene before us. The light of the moon casts a silver sheen across a swath of the great lake. Waves rise and fall darkly, like the hulking shapes of sea creatures, arching their backs above the water.

"What do you think?" asks J.D.

I look long and hard and see for myself that it's real and good. I try to believe that there's too much water here for Thorne to permanently taint, but I know better. This lake had been full once before, and it had turned to poison and then to dust.

"Life finds a way, J.D. That's what I was thinking." I say softly. "I know Thorne is going to try and make this water work for his purposes. And I know there are no living things in the lake. No fish. No plants. But I believe life finds a way. And making this water was a good thing." My gaze at the lake is wistful. "We're covered in mud, J.D., do you think we have time for...."

"No."

I can't resist making a face. J.D. laughs, giving my hand a squeeze, and we set out.

22

"Where should we go?" I tighten the pack on my shoulders and pick up my step to keep pace with J.D. It occurs to me now that in all our weeks of preparation for this moment, we'd overlooked one important thing. Where do we go from here?

"Northwest," he says softly.

"Any particular reason?"

"It's desolate for thousands of miles. Not a single Biosphere between here and the mountains."

"Why not?"

"It's too far interior. Most Biospheres have some proximity to shorelines, to desalinization plants or easy access to water pipelines. If I'm Thorne, I'm thinking there's nothing in that direction to attract us and everything to discourage us. So his search may not be as thorough in that area."

"What if we stayed close to the lake? We could follow the shore north. We could keep an eye on things, you know? See what's going on. See if there are Territory officials around. Or travelers. People are bound to show up once word gets out that the lake is full."

It's dark, but I can feel the look he sends in my direction. "I think avoiding Territory officials should be one of our top priorities, Kira, not spying on them."

He's right, and I know it. It's just that I don't want to leave the water. It brings freshness to the air, and the sight of it, even gray and choppy, fills me with a sense of calm. But J.D. is thinking logically.

So we leave the lake and strike out cross-country.

Our time spent getting into shape serves us well. We walk quickly, breathing easily as we skirt former thoroughfares in favor of off-the-beaten-track pathways. We use the dark to put distance between us and the city.

When the sun begins to rise, we hide in an abandoned house, one of thousands of look-alike suburban dwellings with crumbling walls and cracked tile. Afraid to let our guard down, we take turns keeping watch. J.D. stretches out his bedroll to rest, while I get our bearings.

The world outside the windows is quiet. There's no hum of insects, no sign of life. There are no motors, no machines. Fervently, I pray that Thorne is out of commission and unable to rally a quick response to our escape. I don't have a clear understanding of the resources at his disposal, but my imagination fills the air with choppers and searchlights and shouting men. I shudder, moving away from the window.

Digging through my backpack, I pull out a map. I no longer have a GPS, so this will have to do. J.D was right. It shows Biospheres to the south and east of us, but thousands of miles of wasteland stretching to the north and west. My heart falls at the sight of the marked borders, the sheer size of the land between here and the ocean. Will we go that far? Is it even possible to survive a trek in that direction?

Once again, we'll be reduced to hunting insects and hoarding water. And now, more than ever, I'll be unable to use my gift, unable to create any substantial body of water. Even the smallest puddle must be hidden from prying eyes.

J.D. sighs and stirs in his sleep. Quietly, I kneel by his side, adjusting the thin blanket. I need to shake off my uneasiness. Heading toward Slag and the lake had given me a purpose. It kept me resolute, kept my feet moving forward. But, what's my purpose now? Staying one step ahead of Thorne? There has to be more to my life than that.

Thorne had said there were others, kids with abilities, not just like mine, but useful nevertheless. Maybe there was a way to find them, to go to the orphanages, to the homes for the mutant babies, to the Jane Does and John Does not yet known to Thorne. Maybe, just maybe, together J.D. and I can find a way to change things.

I jerk suddenly as my body, heavy with exhaustion slips sideways, and I force myself upright. I am completely spent. Knowing it's reckless to sleep, to not keep watch for a search party, I get up and take one more glance around the perimeter of the property. Nothing's changed. Everything is quiet. I don't want to wake J.D. I know he's exhausted. We both are. Moving back to his side, I roll out my mat and sleep.

Three hours later, I'm awake. I wipe the sleep from my eyes and turn to check on J.D. He snores gently, his mouth half open, one arm flung above his head. The casual disarray of his body brings a smile to my lips. I hate to disturb him, but it's time. Shaking his shoulder gently, I wake him. We share a veggie bar and a handful of hemp nuts. Clearing a small place outside, I risk making water, just a small trench to allow us to fill our water bottles. I'm getting better at it, at judging my ability and using it to my advantage.

Afterwards, J.D. fills the damp hole with dirt then covers the spot with old shingles and other debris found lying around the yard. Any residual dampness will dry quickly in this heat. Nevertheless, we don't want to run the risk of it being found.

After an uneventful night trekking through suburban ruins, we spend the following day in an abandoned grocery, surrounded by bare shelves and empty vending machines. It's here that we encounter our searchers. I'm asleep when they arrive.

"Kira, wake up!"

Instantly, I'm alert. "Is it Thorne?"

"I hear motors."

I hold my breath, straining to capture a sound. J.D.'s right. There's something out there, a distant hum. Quickly, I roll up my mat and gather my pack. "Did you see anything?"

"Whoever's out there is too far away. I can't tell if it's choppers or rovers."

"Or something else entirely."

I study the area around us. The floor where my mat was lying looks too clean. I kick up some dust and knock over a wire stand. "That's better."

J.D. takes my pack and we head to the back of the store, making sure to leave no footprints. There was a reason why we chose to rest here. It has an underground storeroom. And with careful positioning of an old vending machine, the entrance is completely hidden.

Now J.D. inches the machine to the side, exposing a faded cellar door. I descend the stairs while he lingers at the top, using a bit of old rope to pull the machine back toward the wall.

After a minute, I hear him stepping lightly down the stairs.

"How long do you think we should stay down here?" I ask.

"I'm not sure. A day, maybe longer. We want to give whoever's out there time to determine that we're nowhere in the vicinity. It depends on how many are searching, but they'd need a day for sure, before they moved on to the next area."

I nod quietly, resisting the urge to peel off the cool-suit I'm wearing. I'm unused to the tight-fitting garment and it feels even more constricting in the close confines of the cellar.

When J.D. and I were exploring the store, we'd come across crates of abandoned cool-suits. They were invented during the early days of the wars, to protect people's skin from chemical exposure in case of attack. One side effect of the suits is that they also prevent surveillance equipment from getting a thermal reading off a live body. So wearing them might help shield us from detection. We've each donned a suit and packed a spare, just in case.

The waiting is excruciating. After what feels like an eternity, we hear steps above our heads. Someone in heavy boots is methodically working his way around the interior of the store, checking out store aisles. Hearing the crash of metal shelving, I lock eyes with J.D. We don't move. Indeed, we barely breathe.

23

We hide in the cellar not one day, but four. It's a good thing, for a second sweep of the town takes place two days after the first one. We have no way of knowing if it's the same search team back-tracking or a second team moving behind the first one to create an element of surprise.

For four days, we live on small morsels of food and sips of water from our bottles, trying to conserve. We sleep in fits and starts and when we do speak, it's always in a whisper.

Finally, we have no choice. We're out of water. Hesitantly, weak from hunger and dehydration, we emerge from our hiding place. Our eyes squint at the dim light in the room. It's close to sundown and after checking the area for signs of a patrol, I find a hidden place to make water. We drink and refill our bottles before hunting for our dinner. We're in luck. We find a lizard and a handful of beetles.

Refreshed, but light-headed from our days underground, we begin walking slowly, alert to our surroundings. A dry wind whistles between streets and tumbledown buildings. J.D. and I bring our steps into a smooth, synchronized rhythm that over time becomes automatic.

Eventually, we leave behind the suburban wasteland for the wilderness. Traveling in the dark is treacherous in this pathless land, forcing us to constantly shift course. Occasionally, we cross an area where life still struggles. Harsh, twisted shrubs and scrubby brown trees dot the landscape. It's not all dead. But the air is dry and thin and sullen.

Days pass this way, in a weary, stumbling trudge. At the first hint of grey morning light, we hide ourselves in some dark place. The first few weeks we're dramatically aware that we're being hunted. At night, we often see the choppers before we hear them. They glide through the night, their motors muted. But the searchlights they carry are enormous, giant blazing beacons that sweep the land, exposing everything in their path. Fortunately, they're easy to avoid.

It's harder to avoid the choppers without lights, the ones that sweep into view suddenly, without warning. We know whoever's on board has night vision goggles, able to see distinct images in the darkness. We see one and freeze, like prey sensing danger, afraid to make any sudden movement that could alert them to our presence. Slowly, we ease ourselves to the ground and roll in the dirt toward some overhanging stone or a depression in the terrain to hide.

Finally, the search peters out. The choppers become more infrequent. Have they moved on beyond us, anticipating us to be farther in our journey than we actually are? Or is there some new search tactic yet to come?

One evening, heading west with robotic steps, we catch sight of an ancient town. Surrounded by darkness, the buildings glow with a soft blue florescence. It's beautiful, a bright jewel in the night. But I shiver in dread, for I know it's a dead city, toxic and radiating poison.

We mark on our maps the day we finally cross into Alpha Territory. A forbidding mountain range looms in the distance. Remote and rocky, it appears uninhabitable. Nevertheless, we continue, making our way into foothills, then into the mountains, climbing up and down, then up again.

Food is hard to come by and we make our meals as best we can, nibbling on brambles and roots and me making just enough water for the day ahead. I'm hungry, always hungry. Finally, staggering, I stumble to the ground. Reaching out blindly, I stuff a handful of dry dirt into my mouth. It is something, anything to take away the yawning emptiness inside.

"Stop it!"

J.D. grabs my hand and knocks the dirt from between my clinched fingers. He turns me toward him and gives me a shake.

"What do you think you're doing?" he asks, wiping grime from around my lips.

I'm so weak, I can barely speak. "I'm hungry" I whisper, looking with longing at the ground. So much dirt.

Or maybe not dirt. Maybe it's gravy or gruel. I reach out my hand again, but J.D. yanks me up and gives me a hard push.

"Ow!"

"Move it. We're setting up camp."

"Now?"

"Now. And we'll hunt."

"In the dark?"

"We'll use the flashlights. I think we're isolated enough here, we're not going to be seen." He points toward black shapes in the distance. "See that pile of rocks? We'll sleep there today."

Minutes later, armed with a small trowel I keep in my pack, I scrape at the hard, packed dirt, searching for anything that moves. I keep glancing at the air in front of my flashlight, hoping the light will attract flying insects. Sighing, I look around me. I need to eat. J.D and I both need something in our bellies.

There's a ridge ahead, and I grab my light and climb the narrow shelving to see if there are any edible bugs. Spying a dark split in the rock, I step through, surprised to suddenly find myself inside a cave. It's dark and cool. Knowing the most delicious insects prefer cool, dark places, my mouth salivates. I hold my breath and listen for sounds of rustling.

All is quiet. I kneel with my trowel to test the dirt. It's soft and loose. I run my fingers through handfuls of the stuff, finding nothing. I stand, pocketing my tool. Maybe I'll have better luck toward the back of the cave.

It occurs to me that this cave might be a good place

161

for J.D. and me to hide for a few days, to rest and recover our strength. We both need a break from the constant walking, the hunger and the tedium. Taking advantage of the cool interior, I decide to explore a bit more before showing J.D. what I've found.

Casting my light cautiously before me, I walk deeper into the cave. It's dark ahead. I'm used to dark, but this is absolute. And there's no sound, only my muffled heartbeat, the faint thump of blood through veins. I shiver, caught by an uncertain feeling of being spun down a black hole.

The thin beam of light cast along rocky surfaces reassures me that I'm completely alone and completely hidden. Resolutely, I push ahead. I lose track of the time but continue forward, brushing my hand against the rough wall to assure myself there are no side fissures. Finally—how long have I been walking?—there's a break in the darkness ahead. So it isn't a cave, but a tunnel. Curious, I step into a thin sliver of moonlight arcing through a slit in the rock—and freeze.

I realize I'm still delusional from hunger, the kind of delusional that can turn dirt into dinner and who-knows-what into something impossible. A flash of pale pink is briefly illuminated as I swing my flashlight around, quickly clicking off the light and stuffing it back into my pack.

I pause for a moment to catch my breath then inch my way back into the darkness, pressing the back of my hands against my cheeks and forehead to check for fever. I don't feel hot. Silly Kira. There are probably odorless gases trapped in the cave, further fuddling my perception. I'm unable to hold back a weak laugh. Perhaps J.D. has found something we can eat. That would be a good thing. That would make me feel better.

Picking up my pace, I hurry back the way I came, scraping and banging myself against the stone walls in the process. As soon as I'm clear of the entrance, I launch myself down the mountainside, eager to find J.D. and food.

The stones beneath my feet are loose, and in my haste, I slip. It feels like I fall in slow motion. I have a moment of clarity when I scold myself for being so careless, before a sharp pain wipes away every thought. I tumble headlong over rocks and ground, gasping from a blow to my side. I try to grab hold of something, but there's nothing to grab. My body picks up speed, continuing to slip and slide until I'm finally slammed into a rocky ledge. Everything becomes a blur, before blessed oblivion.

24

When I regain consciousness, the sun is beating down upon my battered body and blistered face. Every movement is agony, but I've got to get back to the campsite. I am frying my skin out here in the open. And J.D. will be worried. He'll think something's happened to me.

Well, it has, I remind myself.

Carefully, I assess the damage, taking a physical inventory of my injuries. One ankle is swollen, and my right arm throbs. An injury to my ribs has me struggling to breathe. Using my good arm, I pull myself to a standing position, trying desperately not to black out as a wave of pain washes over me.

Limping slowly, in an awkward half hop, I head—carefully this time—toward where I think the campsite is located. Several times, I stop to catch my breath and clear my vision. There's a dull roaring in my ears and I nearly faint from the pain and the heat. At least, it's taken my mind off the hunger.

Hearing my name, I grab a nearby rock for support and gasp for air.

"J.D!" I wheeze. "Over here."

I hear him racing across the rocks and would laugh with relief if it didn't hurt so much. He darts around the boulder, sees me and grabs hold, squeezing tightly.

I yelp.

"Oh." He springs back.

"Gently," I gasp, nearly done in by the pressure against my ribs. I catch a glimpse of his face. Are those tear tracks?

"You're a mess," he says, clearing his throat. He gives a searching look up and down my body then takes my strong side, bracing me with one arm. "What happened?"

"I slipped," I tell him, feeling foolish. I don't tell him about my lightheaded hallucination in the cave. Or that my hunt for food turned up nothing. I have been silly and careless, and I nearly got myself killed. That is embarrassment enough.

Carefully, he rubs his hand over my shoulders and back checking for injuries. "I looked for you all over the mountain. Don't do that again."

"I had no intention of doing it the first time."

With his help, I make it back to our camp where I drain every drop of water from both bottles. Sighing, I stretch out on the bedroll while J.D. digs out first-aid supplies from his pack. I apply aloe to my blisters and antibiotic cream to scrapes and cuts. Then J.D. wraps my ribs, biting his lip when I'm unable to hold back a gasp of pain. There's just enough bandage left for my ankle, which he holds carefully, elevating it in his lap. Do his fingers tremble slightly as he winds the material

165

around my foot and ankle? I could be mistaken. I'm tired, so tired.

"How's your arm?"

"Just bruised, I think. It'll be okay."

"Want to tell me what happened?"

"Later," I say weakly. "I'll tell you later. Right now, I want to not speak, to not even move, for about twenty-four hours."

He helps me get comfortable, shifting the bedroll with me on it into a protected area beneath the largest boulder where it's shady. As he pulls back, I'm startled by a quick brush of lips across my cheek.

"Oh." I stare at him with wide eyes, and he stares back, looking as surprised as I feel.

He gives me an awkward grin and fakes a soft jab to my good shoulder. Too tired, too sore and definitely too hungry to muster a response, I lean my head back on the ground and close my eyes.

Over the next few days, J.D. rarely leaves my side except to hunt for food. After I've rested, I locate a small depression in the ground nearby that's ideal for a pool of water, and we're both able to hydrate ourselves. Gradually, I gather my strength. By the end of the week, I can assist with small tasks. J.D. finds tumbleweeds, which we chop into a salad, along with bristle grass and ants or locusts. I'm even able to collect enough dry grass seeds to grind into a gray mush that's tasteless, but filling.

Now, with a fresh energy I haven't felt in days, I want to test myself. The sun's not fully up yet. It's light enough to explore, but not so hot that the exertion will sap my strength.

"J.D., there's a patch of roots a bit south of here. I'm going to head down and dig up a few before it gets too hot."

"Don't overdo it. If they're rooted too deeply, come get me, and I'll help you."

It's the kind of statement that used to irritate me, the implication that I couldn't do it on my own. Now, I appreciate the offer of assistance.

"Will do."

It feels good to stretch my legs. And the patch of roots turns out to be even better than I'd hoped. I've got several tasty specimens removed from the ground when a noise reaches my ear that halts my hand in mid-air. Barely breathing, I strain my ears, wanting to be certain. I'm not wrong. There are voices coming up the mountain.

Quietly, I pocket my trowel, grab the roots and head back to camp. As I approach, J.D. looks like he's going to speak. I hold my finger to my lips and tiptoe closer. "Two voices," I whisper. "Heading this way."

Without a word, he begins packing up our stuff. I assist, stuffing the roots and trowel into my bag. We quickly tie up our bedrolls, scuff the ground a bit and head for higher ground. The pool still has water in it, but we grab tumbleweeds and camouflage it as best we can.

From a higher vantage point, we crawl out onto a flat ledge and peer between the rocks.

J.D. leans close. "Could you hear what they were saying?"

"Not really," I whisper. "But there was something..."

"Territory?"

"I don't think so. I didn't get the impression they were a search party, more like they were travelers."

Suddenly, a sound reaches our ears. J.D. listens intently. With a small gesture, he inches us back to ensure we're hidden. For a minute, we lay there listening quietly, barely breathing, as the voices come closer. I only hear two speakers. Could there be more?

A micro-expression crosses J.D.'s face then he lifts his head and peers through the rocks. "No way," he whispers.

"What?"

I'm stunned to see him stand and gaze down the mountain. The voices have stopped. He lifts one arm in a wave. With his other, he reaches down and helps me to my feet. Before me is a welcome sight beyond my happiest dreams.

Clambering over rocks below us are two figures, male and female. Immediately, I recognize Tuck and Tamara. I grab hold of J.D.'s hand. "Where's Shay?"

25

Carefully, we climb down from our perch and approach the couple waiting for us. They are dusty, thinner and older than when I saw them last in Bio-4. Do we look like that to them? Like parched ghosts?

When Tamara's eyes meet mine, they are dry, but filled with a grief so vast I know without words Shay is gone. I've never been a hugger. Then again, I haven't exactly had people in my life I wanted close. At this moment, the only right thing in the world is to reach out to my friend and hold on, oblivious to the quiet words Tuck and J.D. are exchanging nearby. For endless minutes, she and I clutch tightly, communicating the only way we know how the pain of existence and the comfort of human connection.

Wordlessly, I turn and begin leading the group to our sheltered spot. J.D. pulls the tumbleweeds from the pool so Tuck and Tamara can drink and refresh themselves. I remember the roots in my pack and take them out now, quickly shaving them into thin, edible strips for us to eat.

Soon, the four of us are pressed together into the

shadow of the rock, shielded from the rising sun. No one speaks right away and the unasked questions are like invisible stones hanging in the air between us. We all know they're there, but we're afraid to offer one, afraid of the hard answers that will be offered in return. Tamara finally offers hers without our asking.

"They used Shay to try and get information from me. They were convinced I knew some clue that would reveal where you'd gone."

"And you couldn't give them anything."

"No."

My heart is breaking. I would have turned myself over to the Territory for Shay. And I know Tamara would have done anything in her power to prevent that sweet, innocent child from suffering.

She takes my hand. "It's not your fault."

"Isn't it?"

"It's their fault," she says, "the ones who hurt her." The steel in her voice and in her eyes is something new. It makes me sadder than I have ever been in my life.

J.D. breaks the silence. "Tamara, tell us what happened after we left."

"These men took me and Shay to a room and asked questions. About Kira mostly. But you, too," she says, glancing at J.D. "I'm afraid I didn't have many answers for them. So they played a tone," she says softly. "It was in a range I couldn't hear. But Shay could. She screamed." Tamara stops, takes a shuddering breath.

"You don't have to do this now," I begin.

"No. I want to." A tiny muscle flexes in her jaw. "Fairly

quickly, they realized I really didn't know where you'd gone, and they released us. At first, everything seemed fine. Shay was scared, of course, and she wouldn't let go of me. Otherwise, she seemed unharmed. But the next day, she toppled over for no reason. I thought it was fatigue from her ordeal. But the loss of balance didn't go away. It got worse. She couldn't sit upright or pull herself up. She'd tip sideways and then be flat on her back, her eyes wide with astonishment, you know how she was."

She blinks quickly, and I don't say a word. I did know. Shay was perfect and completely benevolent. And she'd been too young to understand she lived in a world that wasn't.

Tamara clears her throat. "Anyway, it got so I couldn't take my eyes off her for a second. Tuck found a papoose for me to use, and I started carrying her around in it everywhere we went. She hated it, of course. Then one morning, she didn't wake up. She'd been next to me the entire night, wrapped in the papoose and cradled in the crook of my arm. She just slipped away, and I never felt it." She shook her head, eyes glazed with pain. "How is that possible? How is it possible that the best piece of myself could be let go, and I didn't even feel it?"

Her voice is bereft, and I wrap my arms around her. She trembles. It seems as if she is crying, but there are no tears. She is too dry inside.

"I found Tam a coupla days later with Shay." Tuck's eyes move from Tamara, to me, to J.D. "The papoose was still strapped to her body, you see, with Shay inside."

171

"I was lost," Tamara whispers, eyes squeezed shut.

"I had my contacts 'round Bio-4 keepin' their ears to the ground for news about what the Territory was up to, you know, to see if I'd learn where the two a you had gone. One day, I get a tip. All the suits have vanished—just like that—headed for Slag and some hush-hush operation. So I got with my boys and pulled together supplies, figurin' I'd head up myself to check it out. After all, I'd been in Bio-4 awhile, and it was time for a change."

"By yourself?" I ask, forgetting for a moment that I'd left the Garner Home alone—and known much less than Tuck did about how to survive.

"You just have to know where things are, Kira, like underground outposts along the way with hidden stockpiles for travelers. I've traveled most of my life, so I know the network. Only, this time I weren't doin' it alone. Tamara refused to stay in Bio-4."

She shrugs. "What was the point?"

"I'm sure ya can imagine our surprise when we reached Slag," he says, eyes on mine.

"We saw the lake," Tamara whispers. "Did you do that?"

Tuck whistles. "Man, when we reached the beach, it was outta control. Rovers dartin' in and out with giant machines, and Territory officials marchin' around with dopey looks on their faces."

"I swam," says Tamara.

I'm startled. "You what?"

"I've always wanted to swim. I sank in over my head and felt cool liquid sliding along every surface of my body. It was wonderful."

"Tamara, that was dangerous." I say the words automatically, but a part of me is jealous that she got to go into the water, and I didn't. "Those men, they were going to do something to the lake. Make it toxic."

"We knew there was somethin' going on, that's for sure," Tuck adds. "At first, we couldn't figure it out. And we weren't the only ones drawn to the water. Even in a wasteland, word has a way of traveling. Folks would come out of their dark places at night and sneak down to the water's edge to drink and bathe. It was, well, it was somethin' to see."

J.D.'s been quiet all this time and I turn to him now. "I'm afraid, J.D. I'm afraid something terrible will happen to those people. They're so thirsty, so desperate. And they won't expect it. They won't see it coming."

Tuck and Tamara exchange a cryptic glance.

"They didn't see it coming, Kira," she says softly.

26

I'm unable to tear my gaze away from the face of my friend. How many times during my escape from Bio-4 and the long trek from Slag did I wish I could see Tamara again? And here she is. My wish has been granted. But I realize now my wish was selfish. Whenever I pictured Tamara, I imagined her and Shay laughing together on their small patch of space in Bio-4 or selling jewelry in the marketplace or snuggled together gazing through the bio-dome at the round moon. Now, Tamara is here. But Shay is not. And my friend has been transformed. Her eyes are sunken, her cheeks hollowed by hunger and sadness. But her voice is still clear when she speaks, her questions shaking me from my reverie.

"How do you do it, Kira? How do you make the water?"

"I honestly don't know. The first time was completely accidental. I've never figured out how or why. I stopped trying to make sense of it. Thinking about it just makes my head hurt."

"You've got to do more. You can't stop now. You've got to help us live. All of us. Help us grow things on our

174

own, without the Territory telling us how many drops of water we can consume in a day or how many beans we can have on our plate."

"I want that, too, Tamara. You can't know how much. But every time I make water, it's like a giant flag waving, saying 'here I am, come and get me.' And they want to control me, control what I can do. Since J.D. and I left Slag, I haven't had an opportunity to make enough water that wouldn't evaporate within a few day's time. You've seen what it's like out there."

I figure the shock of seeing Tamara and Tuck is starting to wear off because my thoughts are finally starting to organize themselves. I turn to Tuck with a question that's been struggling for formation since I first saw them on the mountain.

"How did you find us?"

Tuck looks at J.D., and he chuckles. Even Tamara smiles.

I look from one to the other. "What? What don't I know?"

It's Tuck who answers. "I'm gettin' to that. So first, we're at the lake, see, and we start noticin' these tactical teams leaving the city. Clearly, there's some kinda search underway. But what's it all about, right? One night, I'm making introductions to folks who've come to the lake, and I hook up with a man who says to me he'd been hired at this place in town, cooking for Territory staff and a couple of captives, a boy and girl. But the buildin' had collapsed, and these kids had gotten away, and his boss wanted 'em back very badly."

"Thorne." I can't hide my disgust.

"So he survived," says J.D.

"Later that night, Tam and I were hidin' under a pier and we see patrols fannin' out around the lake, chasin' lurkers and broadcasting that their oh-so-sophisticated machinery had detected deadly toxins in the lake. They said there'd been some kind of underground rupture that had pushed all this bad water to the surface of the earth, and it could generate somethin' highly contagious, like a plague. They said the Territory was takin' steps to protect everybody. For their own safety and the safety of others, people were being forced to evacuate the area.

"Clearly somethin' sneaky was going on, so we hunkered down to see what would happen next."

I can tell that whatever it is Tuck's about to say, it's going to be bad. "Electric fences?"

He shakes his head. "Buried mines."

I knew Thorne was evil, but still...the news is staggering. Tamara squeezes my hand. "I'm sorry, Kira. But Tuck is right. I wouldn't have believed it if I hadn't seen it for myself. They were burying landmines along the shoreline. All it would take is a couple of people getting blown up as they try to approach the water."

J.D. finishes her thought. "And the Territory gets to keep the water for themselves."

"I'm afraid so. Occasionally, people will still try, of course, thinking they've figured out a way to do it and not get caught. But most people will accept their rations meekly and just leave it alone."

I drop my head into my hands, certain that whatever

naked expression shows on my face right now must be ugly and hateful. I want to do violence. I want to hurt Thorne. There is no reasoning in the world to justify his actions. That water should be saving lives. Lots of lives, not just the ones Thorne deems worthy.

Softly, Tuck resumes his story. "Some of us didn't believe the water was toxic, see, because we'd been drinkin it. We'd even been in it. But once we realized they was blockin' access, a bunch of us began fillin' as many containers as we could find for storing underground: tubs and tanks and barrels and bottles and small, clay jugs. For several nights, we did little else but pipe water outta that lake. But between the mines and the sentries, it kept gettin' harder and harder to find a safe place to draw the water. And soon enough, people started gettin' blown up. And pieces of them were left behind on the beaches as a warning to others."

I stare at Tuck unable to fathom such an abomination.

"We could tell time was running out, so Tam and I, we boogied out of there. My first goal was just to head in a direction not overrun with search parties. It didn't occur to me 'til later that I was followin' in your footsteps."

"You saw one of my marks?" says J.D.

Tuck nods.

I glance from one to the other. "What are you talking about? What mark? Why don't I know about a mark?"

"It's something Tuck and I used to do back in Gamma. There was a group of us actually."

"We called ourselves The Lost Boys."

J.D. looks at me. "Each of us had a small stamp we

carried. We'd use it to mark a good hiding place or to secretly indicate that a valuable cache was nearby. We'd place the mark somewhere that wasn't obvious, but not completely hidden either, beneath a metal strut or inside the corner of a concrete block, for example."

"And you were doing this the whole time we were walking?"

"I didn't start doing it right away. It was actually several days after we'd left Slag that I started leaving the mark behind. It's an old habit. I'm not even sure why I picked it up again. Maybe I wanted to mark our way back, in case we ever decided to return."

"What if Thorne's men found your mark?"

"It wouldn't mean anything to them. There's nothing about it that would tie the mark to me or that would have meaning for anyone unless you were someone who I'd traveled with in the past and you knew me, specifically."

Tuck nods. "There are actually lots of marks out there you know. I come across them now and again. But once I recognized yours, I started looking for your mark along the way. Often, that was our cue to stop and rest for the day." He scratches his nose and blinks at us. His eyes contain a grin for the strange circumstances in which we find ourselves. "Sometimes I couldn't find it, and I'd backtrack and try a new direction. Reconnoiter. Dodge the occasional search party, of course."

"It's pretty rugged terrain." J.D. replies.

"I don't know how you survived," I add. "We nearly didn't."

"Actually, sometimes you helped us." he says.

He chuckles at the baffled expression on my face.

"By now, I was startin' to figure out a few things, Kira. Like that you had a habit of makin' small pools of water and coverin' 'em up. They were well hidden, by the way. I'm sure we missed a lot of them. Or they were dried and gone by the time we passed by. We'd go days without finding one of them—maybe just a patch a damp ground, and we'd suck on the mud for the moisture that was there—but every now and then, I'd shove aside a piece of rusted metal siding, and there'd be the remains of a little trough of water like a gift."

"I was trying to be so careful," I tell him, frowning. "I wouldn't even make water unless I absolutely had to in order to survive. Do you think any of the searchers found my water?"

"I think you'd a known it by now if they had. Keep in mind that we'd already figured out we were on your trail because of J.D.'s mark. Unless the search parties had someone with them who'd really traveled, who'd been out in the wasteland for months or years on their own building trust with other travelers and learning to see things in a certain way, I'm not sure they would a seen what I did. Sometimes I'd look at an area and just know that something had been moved recently without even understanding why I was so sure of it. Things have a way of breaking apart or fallin down, and sometimes a piece of debris just didn't seem to fit."

"And here, I thought I was being so clever."

"Survivin's what I do best, Kira. But I don't do it on

179

my own. No traveler does. We look after each other. Sometimes Tam and I'd stumble into an outpost feeling like we was mere seconds from death's door, our tongues so swollen from lack of food we couldn't speak even, but we always managed to find sustenance when we needed it."

I remembered the same feeling in those days and weeks right after I'd walked away from the Garner Home. "I used to come across lonely dwellings when I first started my journey. I always felt guilty for taking food from someone's pantry. But I had no idea there were hidden caches of supplies." I glance at J.D. "Did you know about this?"

"Yes."

My mouth drops.

"Anyone who travels eventually learns about their existence, Kira. But these outposts are constantly shifting, relocating as supplies run out of one place and get stocked in another. It had been my plan that before we left Bio-4, I'd have Tuck scout out the nearest underground network for us to use on the next stage of our journey."

"There's a network?"

"There are several, actually. You have to have GPS, for one thing. There's a remote access key that grants entry into the network. The number on the key changes constantly. You can only receive a key from another traveler. And even if you have a key to log on to the network, there's a vetting process. Once that's done, you can download a list of latitudes and longitudes where supplies have been stockpiled, mostly stolen from the territory or sometimes old deposits left from the war. Once a cache has been depleted, it's removed from the list. And new ones get added all the time either from hijacked shipments or black marketeering. Once you've got the key, you have a better chance of finding food and water when it's needed."

"Why didn't you have one?"

"I do have one. But we left Bio-4 in such a hurry; there wasn't time to get into the net to access new information. And then you lost your GPS when your backpack was stolen. And..."

"And?"

"I knew you could make our water."

"Oh."

"Besides, even travelers can't always be trusted. Lists can be confiscated, or deals struck. Sometimes, caches are captured by the territory or by bandits. If the territory knew about any of these outposts and were watching them, we'd be caught."

I nod my head, accepting the truth of his statement. I know a little more now about risk and danger, about the frailty of human nature. But human weakness and betrayal is not the whole story. There are those who are steadfast. Like J.D. Like Tuck and Tamara. It seems miraculous that all four of us are here together in this dry, lonely place. It's good to have companions such as these, good and rare. And crowded, I realize suddenly. This little outcropping of rocks is not going to be roomy enough to shelter all four of us.

"We're going to need a better place to shelter during the day, someplace more protected," I tell them.

J.D. looks at me curiously. "Do you have a particular place in mind?"

"I do."

27

The four of us gather our backpacks and climb the mountain. J.D. stays by my side to offer assistance, but I'm nearly well now. I breathe easily, and if my ankle gives me an occasional twinge, I ignore it.

When we get to the cleft in the rock, J.D. enters first, his flashlight shining onto dry walls.

"It's a cave?" asks Tamara.

"A tunnel, actually," I tell her, not quite sure myself. I take a good look around the area where we're standing. There's plenty of room for the four of us to stretch out our bedrolls during the day without crowding each other.

"Have you gone through it?" asks Tuck, peering into the darkness.

"Once."

"This is the perfect place to conceal a cache of supplies," he remarks. "Did you go all the way to the end? Did you find anything? Crates? Barrels? The bones of old travelers?"

"Flowers."

They all look at me like I'm crazy. "What did you say?"

I shrug, embarrassed that I let that slip. "I think there may be gases trapped deep inside this place. I got a little dizzy last time. However, we're probably fine as long as we stay near the entrance."

Tamara touches my arm. "Kira, tell me about the flowers."

I'm uncomfortable with her question. "There's not much to tell. It was some sort of flashback, I think. You see, I had a flower when I was at the Garner Home for Girls. I watered it and took care of it. It's how I found out I could...."

J.D. interrupts. "Kira, tell us what you found when you explored the cave."

"Oh. Well. I was hungry, very hungry that day, and feeling more lightheaded than usual. I remember walking for a long time, and then there was moonlight coming into the tunnel, and I saw flowers. Not just one, like I had before, but masses of them. It was a hallucination. I'm sure of it." I see the way they're all looking at me. "I wasn't well."

Tuck looks at J.D. "It's a good idea to see where this place leads us. What do you say we check it out?"

"I'm coming with you," I tell them.

"Me, too," adds Tamara.

"Grab your flashlights," J.D. says. "And you might as well bring your packs, too. Just to be safe."

The darkness seems to go on forever. I'd forgotten how deep this place was. Did I really walk through here alone? Even now, with the thin beams of our flashlights guiding our way, the darkness is oppressive. J.D.'s hand brushes against mine, and I'm comforted.

Finally, we glimpse a light ahead. I was right. It is a tunnel. J.D. snaps off his flashlight, and the rest of us do the same. Cautiously, we move forward.

And step into wonder.

There are clouds. Huge mountains of clouds skirt the horizon to the highest reaches of the sky. I wipe my hands across my eyes, but when I pull my hands away, the clouds are still there. It's not a mirage. It's not a hallucination brought on by stress and hunger and toxic fumes. I can't believe J.D and I have been huddling under a rock for the past few days when we had this just through the mountain.

There are thin wispy clouds, the kind that look like white brushstrokes on blue canvas. There are thick clouds, clouds of substance. There are puffs and streams and swirls of purest white.

I turn to the others. They're all silent, even Tuck, his eyes round in a face full of astonishment.

"Do you see this?" J.D. whispers.

I nod, but can't speak. My throat's choked, and tears slip silently down my cheeks. For here, there are flowers. Not imaginary bouquets. And not one lone bloom, struggling to survive, but a vibrant meadow full of them as far as the eye can see.

After a moment, the four of us take off running, whooping and hollering as we race out of the mountain and down the hill. My ankle protests, and even knowing it's sure to be swollen later, I don't care. I have to run. The air is clean here. I can feel it. It's air meant for breathing, for tasting. Who knew air could be so delicious? We run until our lungs give out. And exhausted, but jubilant, we enter the small valley, finding green, finding life. Small insects dance in the air. Clusters of flowers dot the landscape, not just the perfect pink that reminds me of my flower, but all the colors of flowers and they are dusted with a green-gold light that belongs in a painting. It's gloriously, decadently lush and I'm giddy with it—the smell of it, the texture, the ripeness.

I turn and grin at Tamara. It's too beautiful to be real. But if it's not real, then it's a shared hallucination, because she's as swept up as I am, exhilarated by this place. It's unbelievable, hidden in the highest reaches of the mountains and cut off from the world.

Overcome by a desire to know what grass feels like, I drop to the ground. Nestling my belly into the prickly blades, I spread my arms wide, wrapping my fingers against the slender stems. I sniff, inhaling a fragrance that's sharp and green and fresh. I roll onto my back and gaze in wonder around me.

J.D. has followed my lead, dropping beside me on the ground. Butterflies flit around his head. Finally, he looks at me, his cheek resting on his hands.

"It's real, isn't it?"

"Yeah." Laughter bubbles up. "I think it is."

Tamara comes over and plops down on the grass. "Where do you think we are?"

"We're not dead, are we?" Tuck asks.

J.D. reaches over and pinches me.

"Ow!"

"Nope. Don't think so."

I rub my arm and frown, puzzled. If we're not dead, then where are we? "The place where the earth remembers?" I whisper, remembering the traveler's stories.

J.D. frowns. "If there's one thing I've learned from watching you make water, Kira, it's that this entire planet has memories of what it's been. I think we're the ones who are starting to forget. We're the ones with dry souls and feeble imaginations. We have to remember that the earth was like this once."

"Maybe it can be again," Tamara adds softly.

"I betcha this used to be federally-protected land," says Tuck. "There wouldn't have been inhabitants here. No industry. And with the mountains rising on every side, it created a micro-climate, a protected pocket of the planet."

"I guess it's possible."

Suddenly, I'm startled by a small, fluttering motion. It's the biggest insect I've ever seen, hovering in midair before my face. Everyone freezes. In less than a second, a darting tongue probes my nostril. Then the fluttering thing is gone as quickly as it came, in a flash of iridescent feathers. A tremor passes through me. "What was that?"

"That," says J.D., eyes wide with amazement, "was a hummingbird."

"No way!" I've read about them, but I've certainly never seen one. Like every other living thing, birds are rare and must compete with humans for insects and nourishment.

"It probably thought Kira was a flower," says Tamara, reaching over to give me a tickle.

I laugh out loud. "That was the coolest thing ever."

J.D. rubs my arm where he pinched it earlier. "There'll be water here," he says. "Should we look for it?"

Rising and dusting ourselves off, we explore this strange paradise. Crossing the valley, I can't get over how wonderful the air is, fragrant and easy on the lungs. The trees have leaves, green leaves, and seeing the lacy pattern the shadows make on the ground, I feel like bursting into song. Only, I don't know any songs.

Thankfully, Tamara does, and she starts singing softly. The rest of us hum along, enjoying this moment of lightness, this unbelievable gift. Then we discover another gift. Water. J.D. was right. It's here, right out of the ground, in a cool, bubbling spring that doesn't have to be called forth, but spews of its own accord. We drink our fill, and it is delicious.

"What if the earth *could* be like this again, Kira, green and fresh? With water and trees and all of it."

I turn to J.D., and his face is unguarded and completely relaxed. For the first time in our journey together, I realize how tightly he keeps himself closed off from others, maybe even from himself.

"Kira?" Tamara reaches out and takes my hand.

"What?"

"You could do this."

I shake my head, gesturing to our lush surroundings. "Not this."

"You don't know that. At the very least, you could

help get it started."

J.D. nods in agreement. "Since I met you, Kira, I've wondered if there are others who have gifts the earth needs. Maybe these individuals don't know what it is they can do. You might never have known yourself, if you hadn't found that flower. But if they're out there— and Thorne seemed to think they might be—then I think we should find them."

J.D.'s words echo my own desires. Is it even possible? "How?"

"We travel," says Tuck, wiping droplets from his chin and winking at me. "If this oasis can exist here, in the middle of the biggest drought the planet's ever known, then who knows what's possible?"

"But there's a momentum toward death and destruction." I say out loud what I've been thinking quietly to myself for days. "Every living thing on this planet is moving closer to extinction. We're all dying, slowly, but surely. Don't you feel it? Why, look at us." We glance at each other, at how pale and hollowed out we've become. And we're still the young ones. "How do you change the course of something like that? What you're talking about—I don't know. There's so much that would need to be done."

"But people will want to do it," Tamara insists. "I believe that. They'll want to help if they can. To plant things. To clean the air and the soil. To work together if there's a chance, even the smallest chance, to have flowers and hummingbirds again."

"You're not asking for much, are you?"

"We'll have to be careful about how we get the word out," J.D. says, ever pragmatic. "Stealth is required if we're going to keep Kira safe. We have to conceal our plans from the Territory at all costs. And we'd need to find an underground way to help the others find us, the ones who have the spirit or the skill to make a difference."

"Then we can get down to the business of healing the planet..."

"...and each other."

28

The sun's setting over the mountains when J.D. and I wander onto a grassy knoll, our hands full of cherries we found growing on a tree near the spring. We lean back against the gentle slope, gazing at the sky. He nudges my shoulder and points to a bank of clouds moving across the horizon.

"What do you see?"

I know this isn't a question about the chemical properties of clouds or atmosphere. It's strictly non-scientific. He's inviting me to participate in an ancient pastime I've only read about, cloud watching. Since the four of us have made a decision not to delay the next stage of our journey, I may never get another chance.

Thoughtfully, I study the white formations. They're beautiful, miraculous. Maybe I'll always want to weep at the sight of them, but that would be a waste of good water. I want to be done with tears, and the day is too beautiful for them anyway. Nevertheless, I consider my tears for a moment, the idea of them, a link to the earth's ancient origins. I'm comforted by the notion that I carry a bit of the sea within myself wherever I go. It's nice to think that water is not such an exotic thing after all.

Returning my focus to the high cumulus confections above me, I ponder my answer. This is a new experience for me and I want to do it right. Finally, I make up my mind.

"There's a grasshopper," I say, pointing to a bug-like apparition that makes my stomach growl. "And that one is a horse, with its foreleg raised." I've never actually seen a horse, but we had a picture of one on the wall at the Garner Home for Girls. "And the shape above that..." I shudder slightly, but quickly suppress it. After all, the clouds are not a psychological test designed to uncover my personal fears and obsessions. Shoving away unpleasant memories, I turn to J.D. with a smile. "That is a man with a mustache."

He follows my finger and nods at my answer. "I see him," he says. He catches my eye and gives me a crooked grin. "He looks funny, doesn't he?"

I laugh and lay back, rubbing shoulders companionably with J.D. as we watch the clouds shift and change. The man with the mustache becomes a cat with whiskers, then a hot air balloon, then nothing at all.

A few weeks later, J.D. and I, along with Tuck and Tamara, exit the garden and quietly enter the tunnel. Our canteens are filled with spring water. We have made fresh trail mix out of nuts and dried fruit and wrapped packages of treats for our journey. In addition, Tamara and I have gathered seeds of living things to plant when the time is right, in a place where I can provide the water.

Our backpacks are overflowing.

"I'm used to traveling light," Tuck says, grunting, shifting his heavy pack awkwardly across his shoulders.

"Don't be a baby," Tamara teases. Then she's silent, the word 'baby' reminding her of who is not with us.

I touch her hand lightly and can feel her smile in the dark beside me. She's getting better. We all are stronger now because we have been rejuvenated by our encounter with nature the way it can be, green and sustaining.

We catch a glimmer ahead of us and pick up our pace. It's not that we are eager to leave. It's that we are eager to begin this work we've chosen. We are eager to travel, no matter the danger, if it means finding a way to make things better. I am eager to make water. But we have all agreed we must be careful. The delivery of water must be strategic, but it must also appear to be random, so our movements cannot be anticipated. Always, we must look out for each other, ensuring the safety of our ragtag little group and others we may meet along the way.

Back on the mountain, outside the tunnel walls, J.D. pulls me aside and hands me something. Curious, I look down to see a soft block with a carving on one end. He opens a small container filled with bright pink dye.

I can't hold back a laugh. "How did you do this?"

"Cherries, ground with rose hips and lavender. I added mint to activate the alkaloids, a little plant fixative and metal salt to set the color."

"Wow." I'm impressed. I can't help but wonder what other knowledge J.D. possesses that's still unknown to me. Carefully, I take the carved end of the block and place it into the dye. Finding a protected place in the rocks outside the tunnel entrance, I make my mark, then step back to admire J.D.'s handiwork. "It's perfect."

"Do you think we'll ever come back here?" Tuck asks.

I pocket my new stamp as J.D. caps the dye container. "If our plan works, maybe we won't need to come back. Maybe it's enough just to know it's here."

Somberly, I take a deep breath and turn to the others. "It's going to be hard, you know."

"Anything that matters usually is," Tuck says, winking good-naturedly.

Even knowing it's going to be hard, I have a good feeling about what we're trying to do. Maybe because I know I'm not alone. I have my friends with me and that makes all the difference.

J.D. adjusts his packs, squints up at the setting sun then looks at each of us in turn. "Are we ready?"

"Let's go give the people water," I say.

Tamara shakes her head, eyes gleaming. "Even better, let's go give them hope."

Acknowledgements

I would like to thank the following individuals for helping to make this book possible:

Miriam Hees at Blooming Tree Press for reading a rocky first manuscript and identifying what would make it better.

Madeline Smoot, CBAY Books publisher, editor extraordinaire and so much more: artist, advocate, and guide.

Dallie and Patricia: talented writers and first readers.

Author and Professor C.W. Smith and the Taoseños: who carefully and thoughtfully critiqued the work-in-progress.

And finally, but immensely, my appreciation to Ben & Zachary for their love and encouragement: always responding to every doubt with
"You can do it, Mom."

About the Author

Denise Getson has a bachelor's of arts degree from Duke University and a master's degree from Southern Methodist University. Her previous publications include business articles and fine arts reviews. In the past three years, the author has lived in Texas, Taiwan and Malaysia. This is her first novel.